The McKenna Legacy...
A Legacy of Love

To my darling grandchildren,

I leave you my love and more. Within thirty-three days of your thirty-third birthday — enough time to know what you are about — you will have in your grasp a legacy of which your dreams are made. Dreams are not always tangible things, but more often are born in the heart. Act selflessly in another's behalf, and my legacy will be yours.

Your loving grandmother,
Moira McKenna

P.S. Use any other inheritance from me wisely and only for good, lest you destroy yourself or those you love.

Dear Reader,

We all know that wonderful feeling of being part of a family—the special warmth we feel in its welcoming embrace, the strength we derive from its unconditional support. But in the McKenna clan three of grandmother Moira's adult grandchildren have gone astray. With the help of her very extraordinary legacy, will Keelin, Skelly and Kate find their way home?

Longtime popular author Patricia Rosemoor brings you the very special stories of these three McKennas in her latest trilogy, THE McKENNA LEGACY. In *See Me In Your Dreams* she introduced you to this dynamic family, whose story continued with *Tell Me No Lies*. Now uncover the secrets and share the adventures of all the McKennas as Pat continues with *Touch Me in the Dark*.

Look for all THE McKENNA LEGACY titles!

Regards,

Debra Matteucci
Senior Editor & Editorial Coordinator
Harlequin Books
300 East 42nd Street
New York, NY 10017

Touch Me in
the Dark
Patricia Rosemoor

Harlequin Books

TORONTO • NEW YORK • LONDON
AMSTERDAM • PARIS • SYDNEY • HAMBURG
STOCKHOLM • ATHENS • TOKYO • MILAN
MADRID • WARSAW • BUDAPEST • AUCKLAND

To Dayton Hyde, real-life hero and founder of IRAM
(Institute of Range and the American Mustang) and the
Black Hills Wild Horse Sanctuary, P.O. Box 998,
Hot Springs, South Dakota 57747

For more information about our wild mustangs and the
adoption program, contact BLM, Adopt-a-Horse
Program, P.O. Box 12000, Reno, Nevada 89520

ISBN 0-373-22390-0

TOUCH ME IN THE DARK

Copyright © 1996 by Patricia Pinianski

McKENNA FAMILY TREE

Descendants of MOIRA KELLY McKENNA

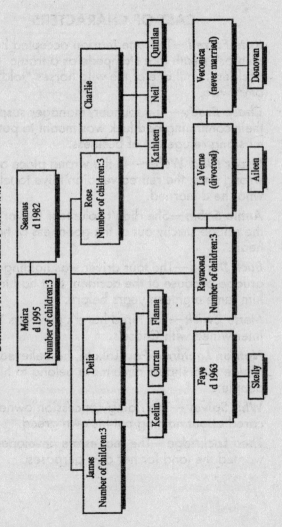

CAST OF CHARACTERS

Kate Farrell—The veterinarian accepted her mentor's death in a stampede as a tragic accident, until one of the wild horses "told" her otherwise.

Chase Brody—The founder/manager suspected their continuing bad luck was meant to put the mustang refuge out of business.

Oscar (Doc) Weber—In the wrong place at the wrong time, the retired vet didn't live to tell what he'd learned.

Annie Sabin—She didn't volunteer to work for the refuge strictly out of the goodness of her heart.

Buck Duran—The tour driver was holding a grudge because of the accident that had left him lame eighteen years before.

Merle Zwick—The hired hand's past was intertwined with Chase's.

Nathan Lantero—Part Lakota, he believed refuge land should once more belong to his people.

Whit Spivey—The riding-concession owner cared about nothing but his own greed.

Thea Lockridge—The real-estate developer wanted the land for her own purposes.

Prologue

The sky had changed swiftly from a luminous pink to a deep copper by the time Oscar Weber arrived at the far-back reaches of the refuge. The flat was dotted with a series of holding corrals, most of which hadn't been used in years. One currently confined several of his patients, however.

Alighting from his pickup, he fetched his bag and a bucket of bribery—sweetened grain mash—which was an effective way of getting the wild horses to come close so that he could check them out. He hobbled into the occupied corral.

A strange sad sound moaned through the sharp tortured buttes lining the flat. Gave some people the willies, he knew, but the soughing wind was music to his ears.

So was the excited nickering of the mustangs.

Recovering from a virus that had spread through the small band like wildfire, the seven mares quarantined from the rest of the herd crowded around him, ready to let him inspect them in exchange for the treat. Few humans could ever get so close. It took a special touch to tame the wildness in the heart of any beast, especially ones who'd already been betrayed by man.

After latching the gate, Oscar dipped his arthritic hand into the bucket again and again, thrilled as always by the soft noses that pressed his flesh for the sweet. One of the mares bumped him aggressively.

"Hey, Sage, don't be a pig." He moved the bucket slightly so the greedy mare couldn't stick her head inside as she was trying to do. "Leave some for the others," he ordered in a gruff voice.

A grulla, her dark gray coat accentuated by an extraordinarily long ragged black mane and tail, Sage was the dominant mare of the band. She was also his favorite of the entire herd. Though some would disagree, Oscar thought she was the most beautiful horse he'd ever vetted.

Craftily taking advantage of his affection for her, Sage pushed at his chest with her nose and lipped the buttons of his shirt. Dark eyes gleaming, she whickered softly. What a flirt! With a big sigh, Oscar caved in and gave her another handful before getting down to business.

At least the mares' temperatures seemed to be under control and their appetites had picked up. Unfortunately a few of the little ladies still coughed sporadically, making him wonder about another round of antibiotics to suppress any secondary bacterial infection. He was still trying to figure out where that danged virus had come from, considering the isolation of the herd.

Only one in a series of peculiar incidents that had plagued the refuge over the past several weeks.

Late evening wrapped the high plateau with its sooty cloak, and sheet lightning sizzled across the open indigo sky before he was done with the band. Sniffing the air, he registered the rain that would soon fall. He sure was running late. Normally by now he'd be home eating supper, looking forward to watching some television in the company of Wrangler, not merely a faithful four-footed companion, but his best buddy.

A howl resounded from the vicinity of the buttes. Then an answer echoed from some distance away. Coyotes. Though ranchers thought of them as pests, Oscar was as fond of the dog cousins as he was of all God's creatures.

"See you tomorrow, ladies," he told the mares, easing out of the infirmary corral.

That's when he heard the sound of a truck.

"What the heck?"

Frowning, he fumbled with the gate latch and hitched his bag and the empty bucket into the back of his pickup. High beams announced the oncoming vehicle's approach on the rutted dirt road. Staying on his side of the pasture fence, Oscar limped into the open. Behind him, the mares whinnied shrilly, sending his neck hair into attention.

No one came this far back into the sanctuary except to mend fences or check on the herd occasionally. And certainly not after dark.

The agitated whinnying of other horses somewhere along the ravine to the south drew his attention for a moment, long enough for the truck to stop and the driver to alight. Senses attuned to possible trouble, he turned toward the person on the other side of the fence and squinted. He could make out no more than a hazy silhouette between the truck's high beams and the hot white broken lines of lightning in the distance.

"Who's there?" he demanded.

In answer, a flashlight in the driver's hand flicked on, the ray blinding him.

A bad feeling in his gut, Oscar shaded his eyes. The mares he'd treated complained loudly. Unshod hooves met fence planking, as if the mustangs were starting to panic. He realized why when, out of the dark, a horse and rider appeared and practically ran him down. The mount danced tightly around him.

"Shit, Doc, what're you doing here?"

Startled by the rider's identity, Oscar had trouble finding his voice. "I—I guess I could ask you the same."

Bits and pieces of suspicions that had been growing over the past weeks knitted together in a hurry. His heart raced and his gut knotted. His arthritic joints screamed with tension. The truth was crystallizing in his still-sharp mind as brilliantly as the lightning flashing ever nearer.

A very ugly truth.

One Oscar knew he would never tell.

Chapter One

Kate Farrell choked back tears that threatened as she watched the coffin being lowered into the grave. She felt as if a part of her were being buried under the glaring South Dakota sun. Sweat made her silk blouse stick to her. Frizzy strands of her bright red hair had slipped from her ponytail and clung to her neck. A horrid day all around.

"I still can't believe I'll never see Doc again," she murmured to her parents and brother, who surrounded her with their support.

Oscar Weber had been like a second father to her. He'd befriended her when she was a pesky kid demanding he show her how to heal the injured animals and birds she found. When she'd decided to go to veterinary school, he'd become her mentor. After her marriage to Jake Nash had ended, he'd offered her a partnership. She had accepted, moving back to Bitter Creek for his sake, as well as hers—vetting livestock was too physically demanding for an aging man with arthritis.

The partnership had been a clever hoax, however, Doc using the lure so he could retire within weeks of her return. All along, he'd planned on turning over his veterinary practice to her, no strings attached. Kate had agreed, figuring she'd find a way to pay him back for his generosity. And now she would never be able to do so.

Her mother slipped an arm around her back. Though smaller than Kate both in height and build, she was solid and steady and comforting as always.

"We're never prepared for death, Kathleen."

"But, Mom, it's not like Doc was sick."

"People can up and die at any time without doing the things they meant to." Her green eyes filled with tears and her soft lilt became more pronounced. "You cannot be making up for things left undone... unsaid... once you're gone."

"You've nothing to make up for, Rose," Kate's father insisted gruffly.

"It's been thirty-five years, Charlie."

Kate didn't miss the sadness that swept through her mother. A sadness beyond saying goodbye to an old friend. She met the amber gaze of her younger brother—Neil was a carbon copy of their father, from his whipcord build and solid good looks to his too-serious approach to life. A man who normally had control of any situation, he now looked as helpless as she felt.

"Too bad Quin's not here," he whispered.

Struck with wanderlust, their younger brother Quinlan was off seeking whatever lay over the next horizon.

"He always knows how to cheer Mom up," she agreed, feeling a little lost herself.

The minister said a final prayer over the grave, the mourners standing with bowed heads, holding hands, wiping away tears.

Not Kate, though, despite her stinging eyes. Unwilling to let anyone see her cry, she distracted herself by thinking about her mother's emotional state. The poor woman was homesick for her native Ireland and the McKenna clan she'd turned her back on more than three decades before.

She was thinking about encouraging Mom to follow her heart and contact her siblings, when a late arrival made her mind blank.

A man *she* hadn't seen in nearly two decades.

Dressed in black jeans and a polished-cotton shirt buttoned to the throat, he stood behind the crowd, enough apart from the good citizens of Bitter Creek to be noticeable. A loner, more comfortable with animals than with people. Always had been. And he had reason to stay away from some of those present, she admitted.

Though his dark eyes were hidden by his hat's wide brim, Kate could feel them fixed on her. The skin on her neck crawled. She tried to ignore the sensation that quickly overcame her, but she couldn't.

Her world suddenly narrowed to a tunnel with her at one end, Chase Brody at the other.

Two decades felt like yesterday.

He was taller, topping six feet. More muscular. More male.

Two decades and he still made her pulse thrum....

"Kate?"

Neil was frowning at her. "It's time."

Flushing, she forced her mind from past to present. This was a funeral, not a reunion. She approached the grave and picked up a clot of earth.

"Bye, Doc." She forced the words past the lump in her throat. "I'll never forget you."

Eyes stinging more fiercely than before, she flung her handful of soil atop the coffin, though with great difficulty keeping her tears to herself. They could wait until later, when she could mourn alone.

Only after she'd had a chance to join Ellen Weber, Doc's daughter, a lab technician who lived in Rapid City, after she herself had accepted the condolences of the myriad people who respected her special relationship to the deceased, did she remember Chase Brody.

She looked around for him, wondering if he would make a point of speaking to her.

But he was gone. He'd slipped away unnoticed.

Just as he had the last time.

AFTER LEAVING the cemetery, the mourners crowded into Doc's rambling old house and filled the dining-room table with casseroles, fried chicken, salads, jelly molds and homemade cakes and pies until the old wood groaned under the weight. Kate had no appetite, but she forced herself to eat a few bites.

When she set down her half-empty plate, Doc's daughter took her aside and suggested she might like to move into the house, at least temporarily, so that the place wouldn't sit empty until she, Ellen, could see to her father's effects. Ellen had to get back to her job in Rapid City as soon as possible.

A whole house, instead of the two rooms behind the practice?

A chance to feel close to Doc a while longer...

Kate accepted the offer and volunteered to help go through Doc's things.

Afterward, wandering through the study alone, Kate considered the shelves loaded with books, the walls between crowded with photographs of animals

Doc had cared for, and every available surface stacked with literature—some of which featured the places he always meant to visit after he retired but never had.

Kate noticed the silly-looking patchwork mutt who lay in a corner like a Sad Sack, bushy tail curled under his body, long nose on his paws. He'd been sick and starving when Doc had found him. He was mourning, too.

Moving closer to the dog, Kate crouched to give him a quick scratch behind the ears. "Hey, boy, you and me are going to be roomies. What do you think of that?"

Wrangler merely gave her a melancholy expression and whistled softly through his nose.

Kate straightened, her gaze alighting on the nearest framed photograph—wild horses on the Bitter Creek Mustang Refuge. The sanctuary founded and run by Chase Brody. The place where Doc had died in a stampede.

She could hardly give the incident credence, not after everything Doc had told her about the way he'd gotten the mustangs to accept him in the few short months he'd been working with them. But the facts were irrefutable. Something had spooked the recuperating horses—the sheriff had blamed that crazy storm—and they'd broken out of their corral. His arthritis hadn't allowed Doc to move very fast. He'd probably fallen and had landed right in their path.

Nobody's fault.

So why keep questioning the circumstances?

"The place could use you with Doc gone."

Kate whirled to face Nathan Lantero. He was nearly six feet tall now, his medium build tight with muscle.

A striking if not handsome man with long black hair, black eyes and a straight blade of a nose.

"Do you ever *not* sneak up on a person?"

"Only when I'm trying to do the unexpected."

She rolled her eyes at Nathan's sly humor. More Lakota than white, having lived on the reservation much of his life, he made light of his heritage when it suited him.

"You're not sucking me into this one."

"No guts, huh?"

"I learned my lesson. I can't win with you."

"Your trying was always interesting."

That was one way of looking at it, Kate thought.

Nathan's father, Delbert, had worked for the Farrell Ranch until his death a few years back. Nathan, whenever the mood had struck him, would sneak off the reservation, even skipping school, to hang out at the ranch. He'd been jealous of her. Competing for Delbert's attention, they'd been at each other's throats from the first. Kate had often gotten into both verbal and physical scraps with the boy, who was older if not bigger. And he'd always had a way of winning.

Too aware of their uneasy adult truce, she said, "That was ages ago."

"So was Brody." Nathan lifted a dark brow and waited for a response he didn't get. Finally he asked, "So what about it? You gonna take over where Doc left off?"

She knew Chase Brody was currently working at the refuge, as were a few other people she knew who'd attended the funeral.

"I'm sure he can hire some other vet."

"Not without money."

She started. "What about the BLM?"

Doc had told her the haven had come into being only with the backing of the Bureau of Land Management, the government agency responsible for wild horses.

"Their funding ended a coupla years ago now, as agreed. The place would be closed down if not for the volunteers. Only a few of us draw a paycheck—me and Merle and Buck. Brody stinks at fund-raising. He's a long way from making that place independent like he figured he could."

"Like that should matter to me," she muttered.

Nathan's penetrating black eyes held understanding. "The horses matter. They need you."

Guilt wormed its way into her resolve, but she tried to ignore the unwelcome sentiment. Doc had told her about the money crunch and about Chase's plans to renovate some log structures on the property so he could rent rooms to vacationers.

"When you finish working on those old buildings, there'll be enough cash from tourists to pay a vet."

"Don't see it, not with the way things have been going lately. Besides, tourists won't be staying on the property till next spring. What about now?"

"Did Chase put you up to this?"

Nathan shook his head. "Hasn't mentioned you since you got back."

No big surprise, though she'd been living in Bitter Creek for several months now. In all that time, she hadn't run into Chase once. Not that she'd asked, Doc had told her he didn't come into town unless he had to. Remembering how badly he'd been treated by the townspeople as a kid, Kate guessed she didn't blame him.

Only...why *had* he returned?

Not wanting to be pressed any further, she said, "Look, I'll give the suggestion some thought. Just don't go making any promises to anyone."

Nathan's full lips shifted into a grimace resembling a smile. "Don't worry, I won't say a thing to Brody."

With that, he left her alone.

EXHAUSTED BY THE TIME she entered the paneled room that served as her living quarters—a single bed was crammed in a much smaller space that must have been meant as a supply closet—Kate was tempted to crash. The click-click of Wrangler's nails on the linoleum behind her was a reminder that she couldn't only think of herself.

"Hungry?" she asked the dog.

Legs spread, tail drooping, Wrangler focused his sorrowful gaze on her. She pulled out two plastic bowls and filled one with water.

"C'mon, you must be thirsty."

She patted the dog on the side when he came for the water. Then she left the room and entered the combination surgery and infirmary where she kept food for the occasional stay-over patient. But Wrangler merely sniffed at the bowl of chow she put out for him and walked away, groaning and collapsing at the base of the couch.

Kate joined him on the floor, sitting cross-legged. She smooched the air and patted her thigh. "I could use someone to hug."

Wrangler crawled into her lap. Arms wrapped around his compact body, she pressed her cheek to his fuzzy forehead. He whimpered.

"That's all right. You cry if you want to," she urged the dog, uncensored tears gathering in her own eyes. "Nobody here to laugh at you."

Remembering one of the things Chase had liked about her—that she'd been a girl who didn't cry—made her feel worse.

Whistling through his nose, Wrangler freed his head enough to lick the salty tears from her cheeks. Kate closed her eyes and ran her hands along the dog's face. She concentrated on the animal...touching...focusing...sensing his grief for his master.

As she'd been able to do ever since she could remember, she became one with the animal, his emotions merging with hers.

A hazy and somewhat distorted image formed in her mind.

Doc, paunchy and balding, bending over with arthritic hands outstretched. He was mouthing words she couldn't hear, but she could feel the love in his heart for the dog whose life he'd saved.

Suddenly she was in Doc's face, making him laugh. He was happy...

Opening her eyes, allowing tears to stream down both cheeks, Kate remembered how deeply Doc had felt about all animals. How much caring for the wild horses had meant to him in the last months of his life.

She *could* spare some time here and there.

The question was...did she want to?

Doc would expect it of her, at least until some other arrangements could be made. Not that he'd ever prodded her to step foot on the sanctuary. He knew what had gone down between her and Chase and respected her feelings.

She might have avoided the reality of Bitter Creek Mustang Refuge since returning home, but she hadn't managed to avoid thinking about the man who ran it. Chase Brody had invaded her thoughts plenty over the months, and now that she'd seen him, had felt the old spark, she sensed it would be in her best interests to stay away.

But she could imagine how saddened Doc would be if anything terrible happened to what he'd thought of as *his* wild horses because they were deprived of proper medical care. And she owed him, had always meant to pay him back, if not in money. Certain he was watching over his old domain from his place above, she was torn.

How could she deny someone who'd done so much for her?

That Chase could make her consider disappointing Doc angered her.

So much so, Kate knew she had to at least check out the refuge before deciding.

ANNIE SABIN stepped out of the refuge office onto the screened porch, a teenage couple in tow. "Head for that truck down the hill," she said, pointing. "Buck's due to take off with the next tour in about three minutes."

Watching from the table, Chase felt his late breakfast lump in his stomach. Not that Annie's cooking wasn't a hell of a lot better than his own.

But nerves chewed at him, and a growing uncertainty about the fate of the place that had become his life had him tied in knots. And he couldn't help but notice that nearly half of the secondhand theater seats

lining both sides of the old pickup remained empty—
and this during the height of the tourist season.

"Thanks, miss," the young woman was saying. She
was practically doing a tap dance in her excitement.
"C'mon, Jimmy, or we'll be too late. Wild mustangs!
Yee-hah!"

She threw open the screen door and ran outside,
Jimmy close behind.

Blue eyes lit with laughter, Annie spun toward
Chase, her straight chin-length black hair sweeping her
broad cheeks. "Such enthusiasm makes everything we
do worthwhile, doesn't it?"

He sucked on another mug of strong black coffee
despite the growing heat of the day. "The horses are
what's important."

She gave him a reproving look. "Anyone who loves
them is important, too."

"Especially anyone who loves them as much as you
do," he said agreeably.

This was the third year in a row that Annie had volunteered her whole summer vacation to run the office
and deal with the tourists, the last being a task Chase
abhorred. During the rest of the year, she was a remedial-reading teacher, working with some of Phoenix's roughest high-school kids. Of average height,
slim and cursed with a baby face—her words—she
seemed a whole lot younger than her thirty-one
years—hardly the type Chase had figured for being
able to handle gang members. But that was before he
got to know her.

Annie Sabin was strong-willed, tireless, and had a
way of getting people to do what she wanted.

Downhill, a good-natured "All aboard!" caught his
attention. Buck Duran was rushing toward the truck,

his limp becoming more pronounced the faster he went.

Shame stealing through him, Chase quickly shifted his gaze back to Annie. "Buck's not going out with a full load. How far down is our count?"

"Actually the numbers are up overall. First thing this morning, we had so many people show I had to add two extra tours. I took one of them out myself. It seems the news of Doc's death has been a boon to business." Annie dropped into a seat opposite him and poured herself a mug of coffee from the insulated carafe. Her eyes gleamed suspiciously when she added, "Crummy that something so rotten had to happen to make business pick up."

"Sensation seekers. They probably hope the tour will take them to the spot where Doc packed it in."

"Maybe we should figure out how to take advantage of the situation, though," Annie said, even if she sounded reluctant. "If we put our heads together, I'll bet we can come up with some ideas."

Chase hated having to open the refuge to nosy tourists at all, but he knew they were an economic fact of life if he was going to keep the place running.

"We could talk about it over dinner," Annie suggested.

Chase knew Annie hated to eat alone. Her being stuck in the middle of nowhere with no friends for a whole summer had to be hard for her. And she was trying to be helpful as she'd been through all the recent difficulties. Still, taking advantage of anyone's death was repugnant to him.

"I don't know, Annie."

"Consider the horses. Remember how important they were to Doc," she said, touching his hand. Her eyes were filled with compassion when she said, "I'll bet he would approve of turning a tragedy in our favor."

Chase said, "Let me think about it," but he didn't figure he'd change his mind.

"Great." She grinned. "I'll run into town for some steaks."

Not wanting to dwell on his circumstances, Chase rose. "I've dawdled long enough." Though in reality, he'd spent time reading the outline on applying for a new grant before leaving his cabin earlier. "I'm going out to work the perimeter fence in the far north pasture with Merle."

"In this heat?"

"Do I have a choice?"

Especially since they had to repair fencing that had collapsed. He didn't know when it had happened. Merle had spotted the downed posts only late yesterday, but considering they only checked the far sanctuary fence when moving the herd to fresh pasture, the problem could be weeks old. An opening that size would be an invitation for a number of the mustangs to wander off the property—if they hadn't already done so.

Someone would have to check the herd as soon as the repair was finished. Several someones, including himself, if he wanted the count done efficiently and accurately.

But first, the fence.

Hoping the physical effort would blunt his frustrations at trying to make a go of the place, he left the porch, rounding the corner to get to the water spigot on the side of the building. There he filled a large thermos, grabbed another of coffee that Annie left on the stoop for him and jumped into his Bronco. He took off down a side road, closed to tourists, that cut across the property.

Chase paid no mind to the ruts jolting him, nor to the dry dust swirling around and into the open vehicle. Used to the discomfort of ranch life, he sped toward the red cliffs on the other side of Bitter Creek, slowing only to ford the ribbon of water that was barely a few yards wide and little more than a foot deep at this crossing. A good-sized carp did a backflip in the air away from the vehicle.

Soon he was winding around hills, traversing a canyon, continuously achieving higher elevation until he was atop the undulating plateau. To the east, a band of mares grazed on black root grass. Ears twitching at the sound of the approaching vehicle, they lifted their heavy heads and stared, then seeing his truck—a familiar sight—one by one they resumed munching.

He took a deep breath and felt some of his muscles unknot. *They* were what it was all about. Taking responsibility for the tough little feral horses no one else wanted gave his life meaning.

When the animals had first arrived on the refuge, they'd been scrawny, ribs poking at their hides. Worse, they'd been despondent, having spent months or years crowded into feedlots. Seeing their sides filled out with flesh, knowing they were healthy and comparatively content if not as free as they once were, gave worth to his daily struggle.

This good health was due in part to Oscar Weber's generosity in donating his services. Poor Doc. Chase's mind wandered back to the funeral...

Kate Farrell.

He remembered how Kate had stared at him—almost as if she'd never gotten over him. Ridiculous, considering how long it had been.

Old guilt washed through him. And something else. Something more immediate.

Despite the familiar ponytail—her near-futile attempt to confine that wild red mane of hers—and the freckles nearly hidden by her tan, Kate was all grown-up. And she'd developed into quite a woman, he thought, voluptuous curves softening her athletic build, wide mouth and full lips equally feminine.

A mouth he'd once kissed.

And, no matter how hard he tried, he couldn't put Kate's dazzling green eyes from his mind. For a moment he'd felt lost in them. Their intensity. Their depth. The memories they stirred in him.

Determined, Chase forced his mind away from the woman he couldn't have.

Overhead, soaring on an air current, a hawk wheeled with its wings spread wide. The Bronco picked up speed.

A few minutes later he spotted Merle Zwick, the hired hand who was as adept with horses as she was with fencing or plumbing or replacing glass in a broken window. Hard work had added muscle to her tall and wiry frame, encased in ripped jeans and a sweat-soaked T-shirt.

As she set a post in a newly dug hole, she yelled, "Hey, boss, you finally rolled outta your bunk!"

Removing her Stetson, her hand protected by a heavy leather work glove, she wiped the back of a deeply tanned bare arm across her forehead. Strands of light brown hair that had escaped her long braid glued themselves to her damp face.

He cut the engine and jumped out of the Bronco, then fetched the thermos of water. "Thirsty?"

"That filled with beer?"

Merle knew he never took a drink anymore. He kept the joke going. "Sure is. Cold and foamy."

"Mm-mm. Let me at it." Slapping her hat back on her head, she freed him of the heavy thermos. "I ran out a while ago." She lifted the spout to her mouth, guzzled some water and smacked her lips. "Never tasted better."

He noted that she'd staked the locations for the new posts along the entire length of downed fence—nearly fifty feet worth— but had only managed to drill a few of the holes so far. Not having been on site to see the damage before this, Chase crouched and inspected part of the old wood, which was rotted in places.

He couldn't tell what had spelled the fencing's death knell, though he figured the wind could be capricious enough to do the job. So could a herd of frenzied mustangs—Doc's death was uppermost in his mind— though he saw no sign of it. The recent rains had done a good job of obliterating whatever clues the earth might have held. Still, fencing didn't go down easy— not this much of it—not before anyone could notice, even if they didn't patrol the north border regularly.

Weird.

Too *many* weird things going on lately, not the least of which was Doc's death.

Shaking away the edgy feeling that not knowing for sure gave him, he rose. "How's it going?"

"It'll go a lot faster now that the real expert at digging post holes is here," she said, her flippant remark setting off a memory that could still make him cringe.

Her quirking eyebrows and flirtatious smile were automatic. Despite the bits of the old nightmare flashing through his mind, Chase gave way and grinned.

Razzing a man—any man—was just Merle's way. Always had been. A handsome more than a pretty woman, she'd nonetheless never lacked for male attention because of her boldness, though he also knew that men used her rather than taking her seriously as she deserved. He had to watch himself, make sure he didn't get too close.

As for the post-hole digger, he couldn't avoid it.

"You get behind the wheel of the tractor, and I'll deal with the shaft."

He never let anyone else near the hydraulic power shaft when he was on the job. How dangerous the equipment could be was a memory too vivid for him to forget.

"You're the boss. Nothing like watching a big strong man working with heavy machinery."

"Show time," he muttered, getting started.

For the next couple of hours, they worked together efficiently, their rapport almost surprisingly easy.

Merle was one of the few residents of Bitter Creek Chase felt comfortable being around, maybe because she'd come from a background similar to his own. She, too, had been "trailer trash" to the town's finer citizens. She'd been without a father, and her mother had had the reputation of being a "loose" woman.

"Hey, boss, did you hear the one about the hooker with the heart of gold?" Merle yelled over the noisy machinery. "She used the *Wall Street Journal* to set her prices."

Chase groaned, though he enjoyed Merle's occasional spicy jokes because they kept him amused despite the drudgery of the work. Concentrating on the job, he suddenly realized Merle was yelling at him.

Chase yelled back, "What?" and turned to see what she wanted.

Only to face his past up close and personal.

Kate Farrell had been an incorrigible kid. Now, in faded jeans, red cowboy boots and turquoise shirt, her unruly red hair haloing her striking features and a dogged expression aimed directly at him, she appeared wilder than ever.

Untamed as the mustangs on this raw land.

As a teenager, he hadn't properly appreciated her potential, but as a man...

Merle cut the power to the tractor. For a moment the stillness made his ears hurt.

And then Kate's lips parted, mesmerizing him. "Chase. It's been a long time."

Gut tightening at the sound of her voice, the melodic tone tempered with deserved sarcasm, he forced out the only return he could manage.

"What the hell do you think you're doing out here?"

Chapter Two

Kate started as if Chase had slapped her. Though she'd been unsure of the kind of reception she was in for, she certainly hadn't expected this. Then again, Chase had always been rude when he'd felt cornered, and from his wary expression now, Kate realized she somehow had the upper hand.

"The woman in the office told me where you'd be of course," she said sweetly.

"Didn't Annie mention that the back road is off-limits to tourists?"

"I'm not a tourist, Chase. I'm an experienced veterinarian," she told him as if he didn't have a clue. Knowing Doc, he'd probably bragged about her every chance he got. "I was thinking of helping out until you find someone to take over for Doc, but if you're not interested, I certainly don't want to waste your time."

She spun toward her pickup, ponytail swinging, but was stopped cold in midstride when Chase hooked onto her arm. Giving his gloved hand a filthy look, she maintained that expression when she lifted her eyes to meet his. He immediately let go, raised both hands and backed off.

"Let me get this straight," he said. "You're volunteering your services."

"If I like what I see." She deliberately flicked her gaze over him.

That Chase was grimy and sweaty didn't detract from his appeal. His damp work shirt clung to his torso, clearly defining the musculature developed by hard work. His jawline was hard, too, even more so than it had been when he'd been younger, a mere promise of the man he'd turned out to be. Natural interest curled through her, tough to ignore.

But she certainly tried, saying, "I wouldn't want to get involved in anything . . . *unsavory*."

Kate swore Chase flushed under his dark tan, and if she hadn't been so angry with him, she might have felt guilty at the purposeful dig.

Twenty years ago she'd been warned about Chase Brody's unsavory reputation—one mostly inherited from his father, Vernon, rather than self-earned. And yet he'd made a point of telling her about it himself, as if he'd been trying to scare her off. Not that she'd ever paid any mind to ugly gossip. That most of the upstanding residents of Bitter Creek had considered the Brodys trailer trash didn't mean spit to a young girl with a mind of her own. Even then, she'd formed her own judgments about people.

Though, more often than not, Chase had been as truculent with her as he had been with anyone else, she'd liked him. She'd trusted him. Worse, she'd fallen in love with him.

Sheer lunacy.

But that was the past. She knew him now. No chance she'd be fooled again.

Realizing they had the full attention of the woman on the tractor, Kate forced a smile. "Hey, Merle." Though Merle had a couple of years on her and had hung out with a different crowd growing up, they were acquainted.

The other woman's gaze narrowed. "Kate."

She glanced at the downed fence. The refuge must really be shorthanded if repairs were let go for so long. "Looks like you have quite a job for yourself."

"I'm not complaining."

Before Kate could offer some pleasantry to lighten the atmosphere, Chase interrupted. "I thought you wanted a look around."

"That's what I'm here for."

Pulling off his work gloves, he glanced up at the tractor. "Don't kill yourself trying to get this in today, Merle. Do what you can and stop when you need to. We'll get back to it first thing in the morning."

Merle's grudging "Right, boss" gave Kate the opposite notion.

Because Merle didn't want to work alone? Or because she objected to Kate's presence on the refuge?

Kate and Chase drove their own vehicles back toward the visitors' center, but after crossing the creek, Chase turned west, leading her to a spot about a mile down the road where the creek curved and widened, and a couple of picnic tables and a gas grill sat beneath some leafy cottonwoods. He brought his truck to a stop and hopped out.

She did likewise, asking, "What is this place?"

"Annie brings tourists out here a couple of times a week for an overpriced grilled steak." He opened his tailgate. "Be right with you."

Kate sat at a picnic table and stared off at the red cliffs on the opposite side of the creek, automatically searching for horses. But the only movement that caught her eye was a dust cloud to the west. She squinted against the sun. The billowing copper-tinted haze proved to be made by an approaching truck loaded with tourists. The clunky old vehicle passed out of sight, continuing in the direction of the visitors' center.

Buck Duran had been behind the wheel.

Though Kate had known he was working for the refuge, she could hardly believe he'd forgiven Chase for his brother Gil's death—or his own handicap. At the time, Buck had placed the blame for the accident squarely on Chase's shoulders. She guessed old wounds healed for *some* people, if not for her.

"Here's mud in your eye." Chase set a steaming mug of black coffee in front of her, followed by several pamphlets. "And information about the refuge."

He wanted her to read about the operation, rather than see it for herself? She took a sip of coffee and ignored the pamphlets. Wondering why he was treating her like a stranger—an interloper—she said, "I thought I was going to get the personal treatment."

He quirked an eyebrow. "How personal do you want to make this?"

Unwilling to play some silly word game, she said flatly, "As in a tour."

"You lived in this country most of your life, so you know what it looks like."

"But the mustangs—"

"All pretty much like the ones we passed getting back here." Cutting her off, he claimed the bench opposite. "So what's on your mind, Kate?"

"I told you," she hedged, having a lot more on her mind than the horses. But it would be a cold day in hell before she related anything personal. "After the funeral Nathan said the place could use my help. I know Doc would have wanted me to take over for him until you could hire someone."

Chase's laugh was humorless. "You may be stuck here forever, then. Or for as long as we can stay in business. We're only squeaking by now," he said, confirming what Nathan had told her. "I'm having enough problems meeting the mortgage and payroll, such as it is. I can't even pay decent wages to the few people who aren't volunteers."

She couldn't help asking, "Does that include yourself?"

"I don't take a red cent—" his attention strayed to a point beyond her shoulder "—unless you count room and board."

Not having expected such generosity on his part, she wasn't quite certain she believed it, either. Involved in fund-raising for the refuge, he surely had an expense account that paid for his other needs. Otherwise, he'd have to be either crazy or the most selfless man she'd ever met.

"So why do you do it?" she asked, trying to keep an open mind.

"That's why."

Kate followed his line of sight to where a handful of mustangs loped along the ridge. Imagining she could hear the natural rhythms of their unshod hooves beating against the earth...their collective breaths blowing and snorting against the breeze ... she was enveloped by a heady and unfamiliar sensation.

"Tell me what exactly you want to know about the refuge," Chase was saying. "If you're really here to volunteer."

She whipped around to face him. "Why else would I bother stepping foot on this land?"

"I could think of a reason or two." He lifted his mug.

Meaning him?

A flush crawled up her neck at the unwelcome truth she'd buried beneath her rationalization. "Don't flatter yourself. I'm not a kid anymore."

"I can see that."

He fixed his intense gaze on her mouth, making it go dry, making her want to lick her lips in the worst way. No doubt Chase would like that—would get some perverse thrill out of knowing he could still get to her on a primal level—so Kate determined she'd let her lips crack like dry desert earth before she'd give him the satisfaction of wetting them.

"How big is the herd?" she asked.

"That information's in the brochures." He pushed them toward her.

And she continued to ignore them. "Does that mean you don't know?"

"Nearly five hundred."

Her eyes widened. Doc hadn't given her the specifics. "That many?"

"Intimidated?"

"You should remember I don't intimidate easy."

Silent for a moment, he seemed to be ruminating. Then he said, "I remember a lot of things," so softly it made the hair on her arms stand up.

"Well, don't," she warned him.

They locked gazes. Nearly twenty years, and she couldn't forget how badly he'd let her down when he'd skipped out on her. What did it matter that she'd been little more than a kid? She'd had a woman's feelings for him. He'd gone and gotten himself into big trouble, and then he'd run without so much as a by-your-leave. He'd taken the trust she'd given him and thrown it back in her face.

No letter. No phone message. Nothing.

That was what she hoped he would recall.

Gratified when he was the first to glance away, his expression uneasy, she figured he *had* remembered. She was surprised at his reaction. Guilt? She never would have suspected he was capable of remorse.

He'd have to have a heart first.

Gazing out at the land, Chase said, "The refuge is eighteen thousand acres plus of harsh territory. Most of the herd is limited to the other side of the creek. Tourists occasionally get glimpses of a band like we just did, but they never get near the truly wild horses."

She heard the satisfaction in his tone, as if it was important to him that the mustangs stay as wild as possible. "So people pay to *maybe* see some horses from a distance?"

"They don't leave here disappointed. That would be bad business, wouldn't it," he said, the word *business* sounding like a dirty word. "I make sure the tourists get their mustang fix. We drive them out to the closer pastures where we keep the adopted horses. Nearly a hundred of them now that we have yearlings and foals."

She knew about the breeding from Doc of course, but she hadn't questioned him too closely lest he get the wrong idea about her interest in the subject. "I thought there were too many wild horses to take care of already."

"A little policy change on my part. The mares that were part of the deal with the BLM have been barren for years and will stay that way," he clarified. "They were part of a sterility experiment using steroids. And the males were delivered gelded. But in addition, I've personally bought mares from the Adopt-a-Horse program for more than a dozen years—starting back when this place was only a twinkle in my mind."

Mustangs continued to run free on federal land, Kate knew, and under the protection of the Wild Free-Roaming Horse and Burro Act, their numbers had become problematic. She'd heard about whole herds dying from starvation or dehydration because of lack of vegetation or water. To keep their numbers in check, the federal government had initiated the Adopt-a-Horse program.

According to Doc, although now only young horses were gathered, during the first several years of the program, many of the animals culled from the bigger herds had been too old, too sick or too ugly for anyone to adopt. They'd ended up in federal feedlots where they would remain until they died. A handful of individuals and organizations decided to do something about the awful situation—to give the horses a better life for whatever time they had left.

Doc had told her Chase was one of the handful. He'd founded the not-for-profit organization that was the official owner of Bitter Creek Mustang Refuge, so that at least some of the unadoptables would live out their remaining days in relative freedom.

Maybe Chase did have a heart, after all, she conceded. And he probably was crazy, too. Hating that she had a reason to like him whether or not she wanted to, she said, "So you've been breeding the mustangs you yourself own."

"I brought in a prime stallion two years ago to service the girls," he agreed. "Hopefully the offspring'll bring in a few thousand apiece—enough money to make some difference around here."

Which meant that, in addition to not taking a salary, he was willing to kick in any money he could personally generate.

In an area where one could get a decent saddle horse for two or three hundred dollars, a few thousand was way out of line, Kate knew. Undoubtedly Chase was counting on the sentimental value of someone's desire to own an American icon and thinking of the inflated price as being a well-spent contribution to a romantic cause.

"So what do you say?" he asked.

"About?"

"Vetting my horses."

His horses? She supposed they were.

"I'll make some time. *Temporarily,*" she emphasized, not wanting him to think she was at his disposal. "You'll have to start looking for someone permanent to replace Doc."

He shrugged. "Right."

His too-casual response made her a little edgy. She didn't want to feel trapped in the situation. If Chase wouldn't actively look for a replacement, she could ask around herself. Maybe she could find a couple of vets willing to donate some of their time. That way, the whole burden wouldn't be on one person.

"So what do you need done first?" she asked.

"You free tomorrow afternoon?"

"I was going to move my things over to Doc's house—um, I'll be staying there until Ellen sells—but I guess there's no hurry." Not that she had a lot to move. When she'd returned to Bitter Creek, she'd left most of her possessions behind in Sioux Falls, as she had her life. "Besides, I can bring over a few things at a time."

"If you ask real nice, I'll help."

Kate eyed Chase warily, searching for motive. But if he had one, he was keeping it to himself. Not that it mattered. Being alone with him in close quarters wouldn't be a smart move, and she gave herself credit for having a modicum of native intelligence.

"If I need you, I'll whistle," she returned. And before he could get a response out of his open mouth, she added, "About tomorrow?"

"We should be done with the fencing by noon. Then we'll need to count noses."

"You think some of the herd strayed?"

"No telling. If you come along, you'll get your close-up tour of the property, and we can locate the band of mares Doc was treating for that virus."

"They're mixed in with the main herd?" she asked, immediately concerned.

"Afraid so. Doc said they were well on their way to recovery, though, so hopefully it's no problem. Even so, you should check them out. If you can get close enough."

"I can."

"Awfully sure of yourself."

"If you'll remember, I never had trouble communicating with animals."

"I thought that was a kid thing," he said, pulling a face, "like invisible companions."

"And I thought you knew me better than that."

Besides, though she now considered herself a kid when her heart had been broken, she'd actually been fifteen—a little old for invisible companions, and he knew it. At the time she'd thought he'd believed her. Kate guessed he'd fooled her about a lot of things.

"Oh, Lord, spare me." He was shaking his head. "Now I've got to deal with a woman who talks to animals."

Tightly, she said, "And who listens when they talk back."

Though Chase lifted a questioning eyebrow, he said no more about the issue. He took a big swig of his coffee, which had to be cold by now. And then he gave a start, his gaze narrowing on something in the distance. A scar above his right cheekbone whitened and the sound of the mug clanking against the table half covered his vivid curse.

Wondering how he'd gotten the scar that just missed his eye, Kate whirled around to see what was bothering him. "What's wrong?" she asked, even while spotting the string of lathered horses in the distance.

"Damn Whit Spivey!" he muttered, jumping to his feet, his expression furious. "He ran them north of the creek again! Went downstream this time, probably thinking no one would ever know the difference."

"You're talking about a trail ride?"

He nodded curtly. "Taking visitors where he shouldn't be and bothering the horses so his customers'll have something to brag about to their friends." Moving away from the table, he added, "I suspect he purposely spooks the mustangs into an all-out run."

And Chase was running off on her, Kate realized. *Again.* While she stood staring after him like an idiot, he jogged toward his truck.

"Hey, wait a minute," she called after him, "are we through?" Obviously they were since he didn't respond. She yelled again, anyway. "What time tomorrow afternoon and where do we meet?"

But she might as well be questioning herself. Seeming to have forgotten all about her, Chase was already getting into his Bronco and starting the engine, his focus elsewhere.

Kate knew she shouldn't be surprised by his lack of manners. He'd never had any that she could remember. At least not with her. Irritation teetering on anger, she watched him tear off in a cloud of dust.

Was it *her,* she wondered, or was it a habit with him? Maybe he never said goodbye to anyone.

WHIT SPIVEY had barely dismounted when he spotted Chase Brody stalking toward the riding concession from the visitors' center, a storm cloud brewing over his brimmed hat. Having seen the black Bronco coming in nearly alongside his string, he knew what was what.

Not that he cared. Defying Brody had been worth the risk. His customers had been thrilled out of their minds to get their own private view of wild horses kicking up their hooves. He spit out a chaw of tobacco and raised his voice above their still-excited chatter.

"You folks whip them reins around the post a coupla times now, hear? We don't want no one wanderin' off." Then he signaled his assistant, Teddy, a junior-high kid whose butt he worked off for less than minimum wage, to take his own horse. "Make sure them animals is cooled down—"

"I know the drill, Mr. Spivey," Teddy said, braces showing as he grinned.

The kid led the horse off just as Brody skidded to a stop before him. "Spivey, I want to talk to you."

Though the refuge manager's expression was as foul as he'd ever seen it, Whit wasn't intimidated.

"Sure, chief." Considering how much cold cash he had in his pocket at the moment, he could afford to be affable. "Step into my office."

He indicated the rickety lean-to outside the tack house, where he signed up customers for trail rides. Brody beat him there, then stood fuming. Whit took his time, dumping himself into his squeaky chair.

He tossed his hat onto a peg and smoothed down his thinning hair before asking, "What can I do for you?"

"You can start by explaining what you were doing north of the creek!"

Feigning innocence, Whit shrugged his narrow shoulders. "Just needed a change of scenery so my horses don't fall asleep on me. That was my fifth ride out today."

The increased traffic was courtesy of the tragic stampede. At least Doc's death had been good for something.

"Look," Brody said, trying to sound reasonable, "you know the rules."

"Rules were meant to be broken."

"Not around here." The refuge manager latched onto a post so hard his knuckles turned white. "I've told you before—stay on this side of the creek."

"This side gets pretty tedious." A few months ago, Whit wouldn't have smart-mouthed the other man, but in his mind the balance of power had shifted. "And my customers would rather get sight of the mustangs."

"They can do that on a tour. I'm warning you, don't cross me on this."

"Or you'll what?" Whit sucked on his rotting teeth, thinking that if his luck held, he'd be able to afford himself a dentist. "I don't work for you, so you can't fire me. I got myself a contract for the season all legal like."

"One I don't have to renew."

"And lose the money I bring in for this godforsaken place?" Let Brody try to find someone else who owned a big string of horses and the tack to go with them. Fat chance. "You need the money I turn over and we both know it."

Whit hated like hell giving thirty percent to the refuge when he didn't even have free run of the site. At least that was his rationalization of why he'd taken to miscounting the numbers of riders whenever he thought he could get away with it. But that little bitch in the office had caught him cheating a few weeks back, and she'd been keeping her eye on him since. Not that he'd stopped. He'd merely learned to be more careful.

"Look, Spivey, I'm concerned about the horses."

Whit felt like snorting. "They survived a whole lot worse than being ogled by a buncha strangers."

"You're right. They've survived hell and I'm not letting them go back and relive it."

"If my customers don't think they got their money's worth, *they* won't come back—or tell their friends what a good time they had here."

Finally losing it, Brody shouted, "I don't give a damn!"

"No shit! That's why you're runnin' this place into the ground."

Whit glared at the manager until a movement caught his eye. Buck Duran was hobbling in their direction from the office, his limp more pronounced than usual, reminding Whit of what he'd learned about Brody's past. Who was *he* to play Mr. High and Mighty?

"A man's gotta make a living. At least those of us who ain't saints like you!"

Brody's color deepened, and he looked as though he was going to get physical. Then he got control of himself and stalked off, passing Buck as he said, "I can always find someone to take your place. Remember that."

Threats pissed him off. Whit narrowed his gaze after the other man, loathing the way he tied his guts in a knot. Chase Brody's baby-sitting a bunch of overaged, broken-down horses didn't make him noble. Hell, that made him plain stupid, and he deserved whatever he got.

"Hey, Whit."

He acknowledged the man who stopped just short of the lean-to. "Buck."

"Annie was real busy, so she had me come down here and ask you to bring today's cut up to the office as soon as possible. She wants to make the deposit tonight."

Bull! Miss Goody-Two-Shoes was keeping an extra-close eye on him. "Probably needs every penny to balance the bank account," he said, barely able to hide his rancor.

"Yeah, the refuge is in trouble, all right."

Whit rose. "Man, it's been a long day." His customers had all drifted away and the kid was hard at work taking care of the horses. "Teddy!" he yelled to get the boy's attention. "Can you finish up yourself?"

Teddy said, "Sure, Mr. Spivey, I don't mind," just as Whit figured he would. Kid was horse crazy or he wouldn't break his back for peanuts.

To Buck he said, "Come on, I'll walk with you." He grabbed his hat and jammed it on his head as he went.

Buck shuffled fast to keep up with him. "So, is Chase on your case about something?" he asked, a loopy smile decorating his boyish face.

"He wants to tell me how to run my business. Don't really bother me none," Whit lied. "I reckon I'll head for town and a coupla cold beers after I stop by the office." An intriguing thought occurred to him. "You interested?"

"Sure, why not? Eating that dust all day works up a man's thirst."

Knowing that the refuge manager was responsible for Buck's being a cripple, as well as his brother's death, Whit figured it would be unnatural if, underneath that big grin, Buck didn't hate Brody, too. Maybe it was time to find out how much.

An ally could be useful.

KATE'S ARMS WERE FULL as she entered Doc's house, Wrangler crowding her legs.

"Hey, watch that, you rotten mutt!" she said good-naturedly, setting the big box of personal items on the coffee table.

Wrangler sat and whistled through his nose, but he'd lost some of his sad air, as though he understood she would try to fill some of the void Doc had left.

She sat cross-legged on the floor and patted the area next to her. The dog rushed to her side, sticking his cold nose in her face. Kate laughed and Wrangler tried to lick her lips.

Pulling back, she complained, "Ooh, not dog kisses!"

The mutt merely became more determined to give her some affection and stepped all over her. Kate hugged him and ruffled his fur.

"Want to help me check out what's in this box?" she asked. "Of course you do. Sit."

With a little physical maneuvering, she managed to convince him to sit next to her. Then she removed the lid from the box. The top item was an old scrapbook she'd started in high school. She turned back the cover and several pages of photographs of her family and schoolmates.

"Do you recognize him?" she asked Wrangler, pointing to a picture of Doc and a scrawny stray cat whose broken leg he'd set.

But the glossy held little interest for the dog. Apparently appreciative of her company, however, he remained at her side, watching her page through her youth. The scrapbook held many memories, including ones she'd rather forget, Kate thought, pausing at a photo of her with Chase. Her feelings for him had been plain enough to see. She wondered if he'd ever looked at her close enough to recognize them.

Not wanting to dwell on her unresolved anger, she continued poring through the scrapbook, keeping Wrangler's attention with a running dialogue that he seemed to understand. When she came to the photographs of her and Jake and his family, however, she fell silent. Their marriage ending so quickly had left her with still-unresolved questions.

She hadn't added anything to the scrapbook since—except for the letter from her Irish grandmother, Moira McKenna. Unfolding the thick cream-colored sheet of paper, she read the missive, which ironically, she'd received on the eve of her divorce.

> To my darling Kathleen,
> I leave you my love and more. Within thirty-three days after your thirty-third birthday—enough time to know what you are about—you will have in your grasp a legacy of which your dreams are made. Dreams are not always tangible things, but more often are born in the heart. Act selflessly in another's behalf, and my legacy shall be yours.
>
> Your loving grandmother,
Moira McKenna

> P.S. Use any other inheritance from me wisely and only for good lest you harm yourself or those you love.

Neil had received an identical copy, she knew—as had Quin, though Mom had been obliged to mail his to wherever in the world he'd been at the time. Neil had speculated that Moira had sent the same letter to all nine of her American and Irish grandchildren, but Kate had been of no mind to discuss the matter at length.

While she'd appreciated the sincerity of Moira's bequest—the dying woman had obviously wanted her grandchildren to be happy, after the way each of her own children had blemished their personal lives with prejudice and anger—Kate had realized she'd already blown her chance at happiness.

"'Act selflessly in another's behalf, and my legacy shall be yours,'" she quoted to Wrangler, who tilted his head as if trying to understand.

Even now, she wondered if she had been too selfish to be married. Maybe she should have given up being a veterinarian and started having babies as Jake had demanded of her. Not that she didn't want kids. She was well aware of her biological clock tick-tick-ticking away. But she hadn't seen that doing what she'd been born to do and having a family were mutually exclusive.

And before they married neither had Jake.

What it came down to, she suspected, was that her husband had never truly believed in her special ability to communicate with animals, but had humored her while it suited him. Just as Chase had. In either case, she shouldn't have been surprised. People who couldn't relate to something beyond their own reality had given her a lot of guff over the years. On the outside she'd remained unaffected by their laughter and derision, but inside, she'd been hurt.

Her mother had told her she'd inherited her gift from her grandmother. Kate had always wondered if Moira had suffered for being different, too.

Her gaze strayed back to the letter.

"'Within thirty-three days after your thirty-third birthday...'" Ironic. "I was thirty-three last week," she told the dog. "Grandmother's timing was a bit off, wouldn't you say?"

Wrangler's tail thumped in agreement.

No man in her life. No man who even interested her. As if to put a lie to her thoughts, Chase came to mind. But he'd left her once and she had only hostile feelings toward him. *Mostly* hostile feelings, she amended, remembering the moment she'd first seen him at the cemetery.

No matter, *she* had to be the problem. Something within her kept men from accepting and loving her as she was. *Because* she was different? She'd had no luck with Chase. No luck with marriage to Jake. The well-intentioned wishes of her grandmother were just that, at least in her case, Kate decided sadly, refolding the letter and burying it in the scrapbook.

"The McKenna Legacy is a pretty tale," she told the dog, snuggling with him. "But not for the likes of me."

Chapter Three

The next morning, Kate attended church with her family and came back to the Farrell Ranch for a late breakfast, a Sunday tradition. She loved the sprawling ranch house she'd grown up in, though she didn't feel she belonged there anymore—one of the reasons she'd turned down her parents when, upon her return to Bitter Creek, they'd suggested she move in with them until she could find something more suitable than the cramped quarters behind the practice.

The smell of coffee and eggs, sausage and potatoes led them straight to the kitchen where the heavy, scarred wooden table was laden with enough food for a bunkhouse full of starving cowboys. The housekeeper had outdone herself before leaving to spend the day with her own family.

They'd barely started passing platters of food when Neil announced, "Skelly called last night."

Pouring herself a tall glass of freshly squeezed orange juice, Kate turned at the mention of their Chicago cousin. She'd spent some time with Skelly and his half-sister, Aileen, while attending a professional conference in the big city. And, of course, she caught his afternoon television show, "The Whole Truth," every so often.

"There's nothing wrong, is there?" she asked, hoping all was well with their uncle Raymond, their mother's triplet brother whom they'd never met.

"Skelly's getting married today to Rosalind Van Straaten, heiress to Temptress."

Kate gaped. "As in the hair-products-and-cosmetics company?"

"The same."

"And he didn't have the good taste to invite his own first cousins," her father said, handing a plate of sausages to Neil. "Obviously family means little to him. Isn't that just like a McKenna."

"The wedding is very small, a last-minute thing," Neil explained. "As a matter of fact, it's a double ceremony. Keelin—" one of their Irish cousins "—was visiting in Chicago when she met the love of her life, a man named Tyler Leighton, and—"

"Her father will be thrilled, I'm certain," Charlie interrupted in a harsh voice. "His Irish daughter marrying an *American* of all things, and, if the name tells, a Protestant to boot."

"Charlie, perhaps James has mellowed," Rose said of her other triplet who'd never left his native land.

"Leopards don't change their spots."

Kate exchanged a knowing look with her brother. They'd heard the familiar argument for too many years. Their father was unbending when it came to his opinions about their mother's family. Though he did have good reason.

Rose's brothers, James and Raymond, had forbidden her to have anything to do with Charlie Farrell, a Protestant visitor to their country. When Rose hadn't complied, had insisted she meant to marry her beloved Charlie despite their wishes, her brothers warned her never to darken the McKenna doorstep again. In turn, Rose had wished for her brothers the same unhappiness they wished for her.

Shortly afterward, Kate knew, James and Raymond's falling in love with the same woman caused a further rift in the family. Raymond won Faye O'Reilly's heart and carried his new bride off to America, only to lose her giving birth to Skelly. And James married on the rebound, his marriage suitable if not exactly a love match. She'd gathered the details from reading Mom's letters from her own mother, Moira.

"Anyhow," Neil went on, "Keelin and her groom will be driving west for their honeymoon, and she wants to meet everyone." He looked straight at Kate when he said, "Especially you."

That surprised her. "Why especially me? What in the world did Skelly tell her?"

"You'll have to ask her when they get here—possibly late Tuesday. She'll call again when she's more certain of their arrival time."

Sticking his fork into a roasted potato, her father groused, "Well, I hope they don't think they're staying on Farrell Ranch property." He glared at Neil, who had built his own home overlooking the creek several years before, as if challenging his son to defy him.

Before Neil could say a thing, however, her mother returned, "Don't you be making decisions for *us,* Charlie Farrell. I'll be welcoming my niece into this house, if you please—whether or not *you're* here!"

Kate went wide-eyed. She'd never heard her mother speak to her father so bluntly before, practically ordering him to accept her niece or leave the house. Her father's face suffused with color.

"A fine turn of events!" he muttered, standing. "Where's your loyalty, Rose?" He didn't wait for an answer, rather threw down his napkin and stalked out of the room without ever having touched his food.

The discord between her parents made Kate lose her appetite, too. "Mom, Keelin and her husband could stay with me at Doc's place."

"I don't need you to play peacemaker, Kathleen." Her mother's eyes filled with tears. "I'll be standing by my word, but thank you."

Neil said nothing, merely poked at his food aimlessly. He'd always hated arguments, too.

Kate tried to smooth over the tension in the room. "So, Skelly is getting married today." Having been entertained with several of his disastrous dating stories—neatly embellished, she was sure—she'd wondered if he would ever get serious about any woman. "I'm happy for him."

"'Tis more than time if you're asking me," Rose said of the nephew she'd never met. The topic seemed to chase away her sadness, at least for the moment. "He and Keelin are both thirty-three—*your* age."

Kate recognized that tone of voice. Dryly she reminded her, "I've *been* married."

"I know the Catholic Church frowns on divorce, but people can make mistakes and shouldn't be punished for them by being lonely for the rest of their lives."

The family's having alternately attended both Catholic and Methodist churches in respect to both parents' beliefs, Kate had never defined herself as one or the other. Religious tenet wasn't what made her reluctant to think about a new relationship. She was only hoping her mother wasn't saying that *she* had made a mistake by defying her brothers, because as she got older, Rose mourned her family's loss aloud more and more.

But all Kate said was, "I'm too busy to notice my lack of a social life."

"So I've heard." Her mother's pretty face tightened in disapproval.

"Heard what?"

"About your going over to the refuge to volunteer yesterday. You could use your spare time to develop a personal life. More than one available man was looking your way in church this morning."

"When they should have been paying attention to someone far more important than me."

Her mother took a deep breath. "Don't get involved with him, Kathleen. Please. He broke your heart once—"

"She's not going to get involved with Chase Brody again, Mom," Neil interrupted. "She's too smart to make the same mistake twice. Right, Kate?"

"Right," she said, even as Chase's dark image came clearly to mind.

She was grateful when her mother dropped the issue and began talking about her bridge club. A safe enough topic. Unemotional. And Kate wouldn't have to say a thing about driving out to the refuge when she left the ranch.

Half listening, having recognized the fact that Skelly and Keelin were only a few weeks older than she was, Kate thought of Moira's letter.

Within thirty-three days after your thirty-third birthday—enough time to know what you are about...

The McKenna Legacy at work?

A chill shot through her.

With her inexplicable ability to communicate with animals, she knew better than to disbelieve the sometimes mysterious workings of the universe. According to her mother, she'd inherited the touch from her Irish grandmother.

But could Moira McKenna really reach from the grave to shape events in the lives of her descendants?

Kate figured she didn't have long to find out.

"WHY ARE WE TAKING the truck, instead of horses?" Kate asked Chase a few hours later as they sped across the refuge, leaving a cloud of reddish dust behind.

They would do a head count as they drove west to the far reaches of the property—the area where Doc had been killed. Nathan and a volunteer were covering the eastern portion of the refuge, while Merle and a second volunteer had been assigned the north pastures, where they'd finished repairing fences that morning.

"First of all," Chase began, "we'll get from point to point faster—"

"Not if the mustangs hide in some narrow canyon."

"Which would be more likely to happen if we ride out."

"I don't understand."

"How do you think these horses were gathered from federal land in the first place?" He shot a quick glance in her direction. "Helicopters spotted them and cowboys rounded them up into corrals. They have a definite aversion to anyone on horseback, as I know firsthand. Several years ago, I hired some cowboys to move them from one pasture to another. The wild horses were panic-stricken. I never tried that again. Vehicles don't seem to be nearly as threatening.''

Chase drove while she hung on to the clipboard and made notes about their infrequent sightings. The herd had spread out in small bands of a dozen or fewer horses.

Leaving her with plenty of time to make mental notes on Chase himself.

Eyeing him surreptitiously, she started with his large rough hands, long fingers comfortably curled around the steering wheel. No sign he'd ever worn a ring of any kind. His sleeves were rolled to just below the elbows, exposing tanned forearms that hinted at his strength. His loose chambray shirt barely camouflaged the upper arm and shoulder muscles that flexed and tightened when he shifted into a lower gear. She'd noted his hard jawline before and the faint scar above his cheekbone that barely missed his eye and trailed into thick dark brown hair.

Now, she also noted how bone-tired he appeared.

But was the exhaustion stamped on his features the result of recent hard work and worry over the refuge, or was it permanent, indicative of a hard life?

What had happened to him after he'd slid into the night like a coyote? Kate wondered.

And knew she shouldn't want to know. Chase wasn't important to her anymore. She'd gotten over him years ago. Long before Jake. That damned letter—she shouldn't have read it last night. All her thinking about Moira's legacy since had had its effect on her. No more, she vowed. She knew Chase Brody too well.

"Wild horses," he said, slowing to take another count.

Kate made some fast notes as they traveled along the flats, including the lead mare's identification number, a freeze mark across her left hindquarter. She vowed to keep her mind where it belonged—on the horses.

At last Chase pulled the Bronco to a stop. They both stepped out. From nearby boulders of cinnabar and plumb, they peered down into a narrow writhing ravine that had been gouged out by a spring-fed stream. A handful of wild horses were grazing out in the open. Chase used a pair of binoculars to search out others camouflaged by the rocks and trees. He was able to pick out two bands, again by identifying the dominant mares. She guessed he'd been around the horses long enough to have memorized their colors and markings. Bays and sorrels, pintos and paints, buckskins and duns—the herd held every conceivable combination.

When they returned to the truck, Chase asked, "How many do we have so far?"

Realizing he sounded troubled, Kate quickly totaled the figures. "A hundred and forty-three. Is that very different from what you expected?"

"There should be more than two hundred horses in this division of the property, and we're almost to the perimeter fence."

"But the herd moves around the refuge freely. Couldn't a few bands have relocated north or east?"

"Mother Nature made it practically impossible for them to pass from one section of the refuge to another. I mean, they can manage it in a few places, but not without difficulty. Plus, we've added fencing to further divide the land."

Surprised, she asked, "Why?"

"Wild horses aren't really wild, they're feral. Their ancestors were domesticated animals set free to fend for themselves. While they've adapted, they don't roam like truly wild animals—wolves, for instance. Horses pick a territory and stay put. That means they eventually deplete vegetation and can even foul their own water holes. They're powerful grazers and the grass needs some time to rebound. So we instigate a migration of sorts, moving horses from one pasture to another. And in late fall when the tourists have gone, we move the whole herd to the other side of the creek for practical reasons. Easier for me to check on them and supplement their feed in the snowy months."

"You don't take care of the herd by yourself all winter, do you?"

"Pretty much. The volunteers dry up and there's no money to pay hired help unless it's an emergency."

Soon they were driving along a flat dotted with sizable corrals, many of them in connecting configurations.

"This is the holding area where we originally brought the horses," Chase said, slowing the truck to a crawl. "They'd been in feedlots so long I couldn't see unloading them off trucks and letting them run free immediately. Who knows how many of them would have hurt themselves in their panic."

"So you started by acclimating them to the area."

"Right. We'd leave a bunch in one corral. Then, when the horses seemed settled, we opened gates to the adjoining corral so they had twice as much room to move around. And then the next. Eventually we left the outside gates opened. They were so used to being confined that it took some of them days to work their way out.''

Knowing that the infirmary was nearby, Kate looked around. A chill whipped through her even before she spotted the smashed planking.

''Doc...''

Chase stopped the truck some distance from the torn-up rails. ''That's where it happened,'' he said tightly. Using the binoculars, he checked out a nearby rocky area that led down to a ravine. ''Well, I'll be.''

''What?''

''Looks like they hung around—Sage and her band.'' He swung the Bronco in the other direction and drove as far as he could, braking before an incline strewn with rocks and boulders. ''We'll have to walk the rest of the way.''

Kate chose to leave her bag in the back of the truck so she wouldn't have to carry the weight down the steep trail. She could always go back for it if necessary, but she was really hoping to find all the horses fully recovered so she wouldn't have to worry whether or not they'd made contact with any of the other bands.

Chase led the way, in one tough spot offering her a hand that she politely refused. He didn't say anything, merely quirked an eyebrow at her before going on.

And when they neared the bottom of the ravine, the wild horses drew closer to each other, ears twitching, noses blowing, flesh trembling, appearing ready to bolt. One horse in particular—a grulla—danced and snorted her displeasure. The others looked to her, as if waiting for some predetermined signal.

"That's Sage," Chase told her, halting in his tracks.

Kate squeezed by him. The momentary intimacy felt a little claustrophobic, and her throat tightened as she said, "Wait here while I get closer."

That he did what she asked without argument surprised Kate, but she immediately turned her undivided attention to the grulla. She gave the horse a whistle, the few notes distinctive and pleasantly musical.

"Sage," she called softly, carefully inserting her hand into a large vest pocket where she'd stuffed a big plastic bag filled with apple chunks. "Look what I brought you."

A half-dozen yards from the mare, she held out the sweet, but Sage merely rolled her eyes, squealed and stepped back. Kate stayed put, but continued trying to seduce the mare with more whistles and offers of the treat.

"Doc told me you liked apples. Mmm, it's nice and juicy."

She continued to talk, mostly nonsense. Words in themselves didn't mean much to the horses, but her tone and actions did. She whistled again, made herself as nonthreatening as possible. When she noted the interest of a little black-and-white paint to her left, she took a few cautious steps toward the patchwork-coated mare, her hand extended.

"Here you go, sweetheart. C'mon."

The mare moved closer, lipped the apple from her palm, then backed off.

Kate sneaked a look at Sage. The grulla's attention was fixed on her. *Good.* She coaxed another mare with a second wedge. Then a third.

And as she was able to step closer to the girls, she studied them. Bright eyes. Sufficient energy. No coughs. Seemingly healthy. They began crowding her, getting close enough so she could touch them.

Taking advantage of a level of communication that had always come naturally to her—if one she couldn't explain—she chose a buckskin, her gaze boring into the alert brown eyes. She inched closer, ran both hands up the mare's neck. Flesh quivered under her palms, but the animal didn't flinch. Murmuring soothing words, Kate closed her eyes and concentrated, reassured at her impression of well-being.

She connected with a second horse and, sensing the same, went on to the others, now walking among them almost as if she were part of the band. Her impression was of healthy horses struck by nothing more serious than a little stress.

Except for Sage. The leader of the band remained aloof, her nerves seeming raw. The flesh along her spine shuddered when a fly landed on her rump.

"Hey, girl, I have a few more pieces of apple," Kate murmured, making steady eye contact and stepping softly toward the animal.

Leaving a few yards between them, she held out her hand, determined to stand quietly for as long as it took. The mare eyed her, pranced a bit and trumpeted a warning. When Kate didn't back off, the mare rushed her. Though aware that any animal could be dangerous when it felt threatened, Kate stood her ground. She didn't so much as flinch when Sage brushed her, the compact muscular body barely making enough contact to be felt.

A thrill shooting through her, Kate turned square with the horse.

Sage vocally tried to spook her. Kate returned with the animal-pleasing whistled notes. Seeming unsure of what to think, the mare eyed her balefully and rushed her again—this time stopping directly before her. She snorted, her breath warming Kate's arm.

And then she took the treat.

"Thatta girl. See, I'm harmless."

Kate produced another wedge of apple and inched closer. Sage stood her ground for a moment, then dipped her head and took the second offering. With the third treat, Kate was close enough to touch the horse.

Already clearing her mind of anything extraneous, she slid her free hand forward even more carefully than she had with the others. She closed her eyes, concentrating on calming the animal, assuring her she had nothing to fear.

But her fingertips grazing hide-covered flesh produced an explosion of sound reverberating through her head...

...horses running...necks lathered, eyes wild, tails straight out... an inhuman scream... the sky forked with lightning...her body being jostled from every direction...

Panic like none she'd ever experienced before rocking her, Kate severed the connection and opened her eyes, reacting without thinking.

"What the hell!"

Sage squealed and threw up her head, then pivoted and took off, tail arched. She cut through her band, her renewed fear spreading like wildfire. The mares whirled around, one after the other, all leaving Kate in a cloud of dust and feeling as if she wanted to bolt, too.

"Hey, are you all right?"

Kate spun around, practically smacking into Chase. He grabbed her upper arms, steadying her. His hands on her flesh seemed natural. Familiar. Unable to be angry that he'd gotten so close, she tried to talk, to explain, but words seemed impossible against the pounding in her ears. Her heart was still beating far too fast, and Chase's touching her only complicated things.

"What happened?" he demanded.

Somehow she found her voice. "I don't know. I saw..."

"What?"

What had she seen? "I'm not sure. Sage was so frightened. Hysterical."

Provoked, she suspected, by an unpleasant memory, more compelling and vivid than anything she'd ever tapped into before. She'd never been so afraid...

"And you *saw* this?"

Chase's skeptical tone gave her a start. She'd momentarily forgotten that he'd never believed in her ability and had placed it in the same category as a child having an invisible playmate. Trying to explain anything to him would be useless.

Shaking off his hands, Kate regained outward control of herself. Inwardly, she was still quaking from the disturbing experience.

"The important thing is that the horses are all right," she said in a voice far calmer than she felt. "Healthy, I mean."

Chase stared as though he could see right through her. But if he guessed she was holding back, he didn't press her.

Kate started up the incline, her mind whirling. What *had* she seen? All right, a memory. A terrible one. But of what? Running horses. Why should that be so frightening? A vague notion made her queasy.

What if she'd seen a stampede?

CHASE CURSED HIMSELF as he hurried to catch up to Kate, who was speeding up the hill like a rabbit with a coyote on its heels. Something weird had happened to her, and his big mouth had stopped her from telling him what.

He'd known she had a way with horses as she did with all animals, but he didn't remember ever seeing anything like this. Her power over the mares had been mesmerizing. *She'd* been mesmerizing, a thing of beauty to watch—not her looks, which had matured from teenage cute to womanly striking, but the very depth of her fearlessness and spirit. He'd caught himself holding his breath as she'd made physical contact with one mare after the other, the wild horses crowding her as if they'd accepted her as one of them.

But when Kate had touched Sage and had reacted as if she'd stuck her hand into a fire, his gut had twisted and his chest had squeezed tight. Acting on instinct, he'd immediately raced to her rescue. Not that she'd needed deliverance. She hadn't been threatened with physical hurt—the horses had bolted immediately. For a moment, though, she'd been vulnerable.

And he'd been reminded of the way things had once been between them.

Then, fool that he was, he'd blown it.

"Kate, wait a minute." He caught up to her before she slid into the truck.

She paused at the open door. "Nathan and Merle are probably already waiting for us."

"So let them wait. We need to talk."

"We can talk while you're driving."

"No. Now. I want to explain—"

"Explain what, Chase?" she asked, using that special tone of hers, layering sarcasm over pleasant melody. "Why you ran out on me? You're more than a few years too late."

Though he'd hoped to get her to open up about what had happened with Sage, he'd known this showdown was inevitable. A matter of time.

"I didn't run out on *you*, but on the circumstances," he maintained, even knowing her accusation held a seed of truth. What had begun as a means for him to prove he was as good as anyone had ended up scaring him. "You know I had to leave town."

She stared at him openmouthed before protesting, "I *don't* know that, Chase. Even if you felt that way, you could have told me. You could have said goodbye in person. You could have called me later. You could have written. You had any number of options—*if* you'd ever given me a second thought!"

Her eyes shot green flames at him as they had each time he'd ticked her off. The memory of those eyes had haunted his dreams for years. But she didn't need to know that.

"I figured a clean break was easiest."

Her spine stiffened and she seemed to grow another few inches. "Easiest for you," she said softly. "Yes, I'm sure it was...*coward.*"

Her contempt cutting through him, she climbed into the passenger seat and slammed the door in his face. Chase figured he deserved that and more.

As he rounded the truck, Kate stared out the side window. He doubted she'd be inclined to do any more talking for the moment, not even about the horses. His not knowing exactly what she'd imagined seeing when touching Sage would eat at him until she'd answered some questions.

Like...did her supposed vision reveal anything about what had been happening at the refuge?

Chapter Four

Nathan Lantero waited for the rendezvous in the observation tower, which was located on the highest point of the refuge. He stared out over the land that should belong to his people. The Lakota considered the Paha Sapa—the Black Hills—a sacred place.

Hundreds of years ago the Anasazi had mined these southern hills for flint. They'd left behind pictographs in the limestone walls—the legacy of Native Americans. The refuge held part of that legacy. The Lakota had been negotiating with the governor to buy the state-owned property when Chase Brody had stepped in with an alternative plan. That a white man had swayed the governor away from his original negotiations had come as no surprise.

Spotting the Bronco winding around a curve, Nathan descended the wooden stairs, careful to avoid the danger spots caused by rotting wood and missing boards. Like most everything else on the refuge, the observation tower needed serious repair if not demolition. And the way things were headed, he doubted Brody would get it together before losing the place.

He sauntered over to Merle, who was sitting in the back of her pickup passing time with Gerry and Lyne, a pair of pretty dark-haired sisters in their early twenties, who had volunteered to spend their two weeks' vacation at the refuge.

"Brody's here," he told them. The truck was just pulling up to the site.

"Finally."

Getting to her feet, Merle threw her legs over the side of the pickup and dropped to the ground, Gerry and Lyne following but hanging back slightly. Brody and Kate left the Bronco. He couldn't help but notice the tension between them. Kate seemed to purposely put distance between her and the refuge manager.

Without preamble, Brody asked Merle, "So what did you find?"

"Nothing you're going to like."

Nathan added, "We think a bunch of horses went over that downed fence—unless they somehow picked their way to the west pasture."

"How many?"

"Give or take a few we mighta missed, thirty-seven in the north pasture and another eleven in the east."

"That makes nearly a hundred gone, then."

"We could look forever," Merle said, "and never find them all."

"We'd better," Brody said, "or I'll have to make a report to the BLM. Missing horses won't look good for us."

Rather, for *him*, Nathan thought. He knew the man was worried that the BLM would consider him irresponsible. The government would have the right to pull the remaining horses still under the BLM's protection out from under him. Then his big dream would collapse.

And, Nathan knew, *his* people would have another opportunity to buy back what was rightfully theirs.

"The horses couldn't have strayed too far, right?" Kate asked.

"Let's hope not," Brody said, though he didn't look optimistic. "We'll have to check with the surrounding ranches, see if anyone has spotted loose mustangs. Nathan, you take the Double K and Rocking Horse. Merle, check with the Johnson Ranch and Big Sky. Kate and I will pay Thea Lockridge a visit."

"And welcome to her," Merle muttered.

"We'll meet back at the office before dark."

Knowing he was being sent on a fool's errand, Nathan signaled Gerry. "Let's get going."

Dark eyes sparkling, she asked, "Want me to drive?"

He was distracted from answering by Kate's saying, "Chase, I need a minute to talk to Nathan first."

That took him by surprise.

Brody nodded curtly. "Don't take too long."

"Let's go over there." Kate cocked her head toward the observation tower.

Curious, Nathan followed. Noting she seemed on edge even away from Brody, he asked, "So what's up?" the moment they were out of hearing range of the others.

"We located the mares Doc had been treating. I checked them over to make certain they were fit. When I got to Sage—she's the leader—the weirdest thing happened. I couldn't really talk to someone as skeptical as Chase about it. I figured if anyone would understand, you would."

Nathan knew all about Kate's being able to merge her spirit with that of an animal, an ability his late father had helped her to develop—and the main reason he'd given her such a hard time when they were kids. He hadn't believed that his father could give so much regard to someone else's child without *his* losing something. And he'd resented that she had an ability considered to be within the province of his own people. One far stronger than his own.

"What did you see, Kate?"

"Running horses. I sensed their fright...and Sage's terror. The feelings were so overwhelming I pulled away from the images too soon. But even with my eyes open, the intensity didn't go away. My heart felt as if it were pounding out of my chest. My reaction panicked Sage and she took off." Obviously still affected, Kate took a shaky breath. "Nathan, I've never had such a powerful experience before."

Wary of where this might lead, he asked, "What do you think it means?"

"I was hoping you could tell me."

"I'm not the one who had the vision." Besides, he wanted to know *her* thoughts. "And it sounds like you already have an opinion."

"This may sound crazy, but I imagined that I saw a stampede—maybe the one that killed Doc."

When Nathan had suggested she vet the wild horses, he'd figured she would be a distraction for Brody. Somehow her tuning into Doc's death hadn't occurred to him.

"That would make sense, wouldn't it?" she went on. "The accident happened less than a week ago. Maybe I should try again."

"So you can torture yourself?" Nathan shook his head. "Better you try to forget you saw anything. I know how close you and Doc were. Dwelling on his death can only bring you more heartache."

Suddenly aware they weren't alone, he glanced over his shoulder. Gerry had trailed after him and was waiting a few yards back. Close enough to hear?

"Or maybe it'll give me some answers," Kate was saying.

Nathan returned his full attention to her. He recognized the set of her jaw. He knew when to back off. No good would come of his probing deeper. But if he objected too strongly, she'd go ahead and try again for sure.

So all he said was, "Let me know if I can be of help. You can always talk to me."

That way he'd know exactly what was going on.

"YOU AND LANTERO have something going?"

Chase posed the question only after they turned onto land identified as Lockridge Acres by a billboard-size sign—and as casually as if her answer meant nothing to him. Not that Kate bought the blasé attitude. She'd seen Chase glaring at her and Nathan from a distance. He'd looked less than pleased— downright ticked, actually—but she'd merely assumed he'd guessed her purpose and hadn't liked being left out of the loop where it concerned his horses.

Now she was wondering if his reaction wasn't more personal. Her pulse threaded unevenly at the thought. Even though she knew she was too smart to be sucked in by Chase again, she couldn't help herself.

She asked, "What's it to you?" and avidly watched for his reaction.

But he kept his expression passive when he took his eyes off the gravel drive long enough to glance at her. "Just trying to catch up."

"I'll bet you are."

"What's that supposed to mean?"

"You never were much interested in anything that didn't concern you directly."

Making her think that she might concern him. Was it possible?

"Maybe I'm not the same person I once was."

Definitely possible, Kate realized, her heart skipping a beat. Chase certainly hadn't grown any more sociable with the years. But maybe he'd changed inside, where it counted. Not that he'd been a bad person, simply self-absorbed. Twenty years ago, she never would have imagined him as selfless. Yet why else would he devote himself to taking care of horses that no one wanted?

When she didn't respond to his statement, he pressed her. "Or don't you think a man can change?"

Irritated that part of her wanted to give him the benefit of the doubt when her rational self saw the danger in letting down her guard, Kate snapped, "In your case, that's about as likely as a leopard changing its spots into stripes."

Chase tightened his jaw and stared straight ahead.

The Bronco was cutting through an expanse of prairie growth, but the vegetation looked studied, Kate decided, the acreage too well tended to be natural. Thea Lockridge had hired some industrious landscaper.

Curious about the owner, she asked, "So what does Merle have against this Thea?"

"For one, she's a newcomer to the area. Sold her house in L.A. and bought a small spread out here a couple of years ago. She's been buying up land ever since. She's in real-estate development," he added, as if the fact defined the type of woman she was.

That Chase disliked her, also, was clear.

Kate was aware that many people resented transported Californians, and not only South Dakotans. Locals all over the western states bad-mouthed these interlopers, who were looking for a better life-style at a much smaller price. Migrating Californians bought up property at inflated prices that natives couldn't afford, after which taxes were raised for all. While Kate figured every human being was entitled to live where he or she wanted, she sympathized with those who were hurt by the situation.

And Thea Lockridge certainly wasn't hurting, she noted, finally sighting the house.

House? Try mansion.

The architectural wonder of wood and glass had to be the biggest, fanciest residence in this part of the state. Actually, with four rooms of the upper story jutting out like rounded appendages—giving the occupants more than a 180-degree view—the building bordered on the grotesque. Kate wondered how many trees had fallen under the ax to build the monstrosity.

Chase parked on the circular drive. In back, showy stables topped by what looked like sky boxes stood next to an ornate pool house and deck. Beyond, another structure was identified by a sign that read Outfitting.

As they left the Bronco, Kate asked, "Are you sure this isn't a resort?"

"A very private resort to amuse Thea Lockridge and her friends."

"She entertains a lot of people from out of town?"

"So I've heard—her way of selling them real estate."

Chase stopped at the oversize double doors carved with Native American designs. He rang the bell.

In a low voice Kate said, "You told me Merle disliked the owner because she's a transplant, *for one*. What are the other reasons?"

"You'll see," he promised.

The massive door swung open to reveal a uniformed maid. "Good afternoon. May I help you?"

"I need to talk to Thea."

"May I tell Miss Lockridge who's calling?"

"Chase Brody."

"Oh, she'll want to see you of course." Seeming flustered, the young woman stepped back. "Come in, please."

The icily air-conditioned foyer was quite a relief from the heat. After getting an eyeful of the interior, Kate suspected the owner wouldn't care what it cost the environment or her neighbors to possess whatever struck her fancy.

"Please wait here while I'll announce you," the maid said.

She curtsied awkwardly before scurrying off through the living area that had to be measured in yards rather than in feet. The decor was an eclectic collection of designer furniture, extravagant artwork and morbid animal trophies—everything in excess. A half-dozen stuffed heads mounted around the foyer stared down blindly at them through glass eyes.

Shivering from a combination of chilled air and disgust, Kate murmured, "I don't think Thea Lockridge is going to be my favorite person, either."

Chase merely grunted.

A noisy clacking over bare wood floors alerted them to the owner's arrival. High-heeled boots and a blond beehive lent several inches to an average stature. While garbed in a country-casual denim skirt and a simple long-sleeved silk shirt, the woman had draped herself with enough Native American–style designer jewelry to set up her own pawnshop.

"Chase Brody, how wonderful to see you."

She held out a hand decorated with long curved crimson nails that reminded Kate of painted claws. When he ignored the friendly gesture, Thea dropped her arm before turning to Kate, her gray eyes narrowing and her exaggerated full red lips stretching into a smile.

"And you are . . . ?"

"Kate Farrell."

"Of the Farrell Ranch?" She sounded impressed despite herself.

Not wanting the woman to think she had wealth in her favor, Kate said, "Formerly. My family owns the spread."

Thea arched her heavily penciled brows. "And you chose to leave that magnificent acreage for . . . ?"

"My practice is based in town," Kate hedged in response to the rude question. Her reasons were private. "Besides, I'm quite comfortable in Doc Weber's old house."

"Ah, then you must be the new veterinarian I've heard so much about."

"That's me."

Thea's interest immediately waned, and Kate wondered who in the world was doing the talking.

Chase exposed his impatience with a testy "Can we get down to business?"

"Business?" Thea echoed, her smile now genuine. "Of course. Let's chat in the living room, shall we?"

She swept them to a seating area surrounding a massive stone fireplace. Kate carefully stepped over the bearskin rug and dodged a chair with a frame made of antlers, a match for the chandelier overhead. But she couldn't avoid staring at the creature stationed across the room surrounded by fancy leather saddles and silver spurs. She'd prefer believing the life-size Appaloosa was a ceramic or metal...but it looked so very real. Surely the ex-Californian didn't have the bad taste to own a stuffed horse....

Thea ensconced herself in the very chair Kate had avoided, her attention focused on Chase, who sat stiff as a statue. He took up one end of the couch, while Kate tried to make herself comfortable at the other.

"So, what took you so long, Chase?" Thea asked. "I assume you're here about my offer."

"The refuge isn't for sale. I've told you that any number of times."

But he hadn't told *her* that the tasteless woman had offered to buy it, Kate thought, wondering why he'd omitted that little detail.

"I don't need the *entire* refuge. Just a few thousand acres of north pasture."

"So you can break up the land into another development?"

"You make my plans for the area sound so tacky. We're not talking about seedy little prefabricated houses lined up like a row of ducks. You should know better, considering the estates I've already developed."

"Housing no one around here can afford."

"So I'm drawing a certain class of people who enjoy the finer things in life to the area. More people with money means other kinds of development, the creation of new jobs. What's wrong with that?"

"Nothing, if you don't destroy other people's way of life," Kate said.

Thea skipped over her objection. "For my next project I envision large tracts of common-use lands and the kind of individual acreage that will allow the owners to enjoy as many horses—"

"Horses," Chase echoed, cutting her off. "That's what we're here for."

"I see." The real-estate developer's smile vanished. "You want something from me when you won't even consider my offer." She toyed with a silver-and-turquoise necklace. "How much do you need?"

"I'm not here about a donation," Chase assured her, "though I'd be pleased to accept one if you're feeling generous." He paused a moment, then when she didn't respond, went on. "Some of my horses are missing."

"How does that concern me?"

"Your property adjoins the refuge. About a hundred head have disappeared. I thought some of them might have wandered onto your land."

She appeared unconcerned. "No one working for me has mentioned any loose mustangs."

"Wild horses wouldn't exactly prance around some strangers," Kate told her. "More likely, they're hiding in some canyon or brushy area where you might not be able to spot them unless you were looking hard."

"Right," Chase said. "So you won't mind if we check around for ourselves...."

"That won't be necessary. I'll alert my manager to have the men sweep the range."

"It'd go faster if I went out with them."

"Not really." Thea's gray eyes suddenly turned as flinty as her expression. "You're not familiar with my property. Besides, I'm certain you can find something more useful to do with your time."

Her tone left no room for argument, and they all rose to their feet.

Still, Kate couldn't help but be amazed that Chase let it go so easily. She would have expected him to argue. To bully. To get what he wanted. This was a new side of him, all right, one she hadn't expected. And one she wasn't certain she appreciated, though she guessed she should. Lack of social skills had always been one of his shortcomings.

"Well, thanks for the help, Thea," Chase said dryly.

Kate touched his arm. "We'd better get going."

But he didn't budge. "You'll let me know what your men find, right?"

"Of course." Thea sighed and her features softened. She actually appeared sympathetic when she said, "You know, Chase, you need to start being realistic. Why, it's common knowledge that the refuge has been on shaky ground for some time. And poor Oscar Weber's death can't have helped matters."

"As a matter of fact, we've gotten a load of sensation seekers taking tours and trail rides," Chase said, though—to Kate's approval—he didn't sound at all happy about the fact.

"A temporary aberration. And in the meantime, serious prospective sponsors might be turned off thinking the place isn't all it's cracked up to be. Not when a volunteer dies in a careless accident, for heaven's sake."

Not liking the woman's subtle derision or fake compassion, Kate snapped, "Doc wasn't careless and we can't be sure his death was an accident!"

Thea stared at her. "But surely the medical examiner—"

"Doesn't know everything," Kate interjected.

The other woman blinked, then snapped her attention back to Chase. "Sooner or later you'll have to let go of acreage—if not worse. Why not act now, before things get so bad you can no longer salvage the refuge?"

Although Thea made her suggestion sound reasonable and heartfelt, Kate wasn't buying.

Obviously neither was Chase, because he said, "The money from selling a few thousand acres would be like putting a bandage on a wound that needed surgery."

"Not necessarily. I can be a generous person when a good cause is involved. I'll pay above market, of course. The purchase price will support your endeavor for some time. The money can give you needed breathing room. You'll have time to find yourself permanent support from some foundation or other. Perhaps I can even recommend—"

Chase cut her off. "Sorry. I'm not interested."

And Thea's tone reflected her irritation with him. "I certainly hope nothing else happens to threaten your project before you change your mind."

Kate realized *that* sounded like a threat. Before she could open her mouth in challenge, Chase took her elbow and rushed her off.

They were at the door before he turned back to the real-estate developer. "Something's been puzzling me. There's bound to be some hardworking, frustrated rancher in the area willing to be bought out of business for the right price. And that'd get you easier land to build on, too. Why is it you want a piece of the refuge so badly?"

Arching her penciled eyebrows, Thea said, "Wild things have always appealed to me."

Aware of the animal heads surrounding her with accusing stares, Kate shuddered.

And wondered exactly what Thea Lockridge might be capable of doing to get what she wanted.

CHASE HAD NEVER LET anyone stop him when he really wanted something, and he wasn't about to start now. He'd just learned to use a smoother approach when it suited him. Arguing with Thea would have been futile, but letting her think she'd won this round should have taken her off guard, at least temporarily. He might not be able to wander over Lockridge Acres freely in broad daylight, but he could get a gander at parts of the back property without breaking any laws.

If his passenger noticed he was taking a road away from the refuge, she didn't comment. Kate quiet—now that was an oxymoron. She seemed lost in her own thoughts and he wasn't complaining. But as they sped uphill, road cuts revealing granite, feldspar and veins of sparkling quartz, she snapped out of her self-induced trance.

"Where are we headed?" she asked, shifting in her seat to check out the area.

"To a site with a view."

"Trying to impress me?"

His wayward mind substituting *seduce* for *impress,* he glanced at her. "Do you want to be?"

She read him correctly if her rising color was any indication. "I don't impress easily anymore."

And Chase wondered if she was going to pick up their argument where they'd left off earlier. To his relief she fell silent, instead, and seemed to be scrutinizing the forest of ponderosa pine that wrapped them in its evening cloak, the green so dark it was almost black.

Dusk was descending, leaving barely enough light to check things out from afar.

A few minutes later, he turned the Bronco into a good-size pullover just before the road swung into a switchback curve. Grabbing his binoculars, he slid from behind the driver's seat. He'd barely lifted the field glasses to his eyes before he sensed Kate standing behind him. She really was capable of being quiet when she wanted.

"This is probably the only place where you can get an unobstructed view of Lockridge Acres," he told her.

"You can see the whole place from here?"

Kate stepped up next to him, her arm brushing his elbow, sending a tremor through him. Too aware of her, as he'd been since the funeral, Chase caught his breath and forced himself to concentrate.

"I can pretty much get the lay of the land. Even though we're in the hills, most of Lockridge Acres is pretty flat. I see a few dozen horses grazing..." He just made them out before he spotted a cowhand ride in. None of the horses spooked. "Nope, they're not ours." He scanned other open areas, then settled on the broken land characteristic of the territory. "Can't see down deep into the canyons and ravines or through the stands of pine," he said of the various hidey-holes where frightened horses might gather. "But at least I have an idea of what's what."

"I *thought* you gave up too easily."

He lowered the field glasses and noticed that in the waning light her verdant eyes took on the same dark depth as the surrounding pines. "That disappointed you?"

"It confused me."

"Why? Because it meant I might be wearing stripes, instead of those spots?" he asked, realizing he was the one instigating a renewal of their disagreement.

She grabbed the binoculars from him and had a look for herself. "Because you're turning out to be more clever than I gave you credit for."

Chase found himself grinning. Kate never had been able to admit when she was wrong about anything.

He wasn't thinking of mustangs when he said, "Sometimes I can be blind, but not today."

Today he could see exactly what he might have had if only things had been different. The wild child had grown into a strong woman of integrity. One who could still stir his deepest passions. Who could touch his very soul.

"My turn to get the lay of the land," she returned, now clearly oblivious to his thoughts. "Unless you think I'm wasting my time."

Chase recognized the question in her words. She was wondering if he planned on spiting Thea and checking things out more closely for himself. He wasn't about to admit that he meant to ride out to Lockridge Acres in the dead of night. Unless Kate had changed drastically, she would insist on tagging along on an exploit that could prove dangerous. He couldn't chance her getting hurt.

He had enough to atone for.

"Look all you want," he said, putting some distance between them. "I'll have to trust Thea to come through."

Kate glanced his way, then pitched the binoculars into the truck before following him. "I wouldn't trust that woman farther than I could throw her."

"So you don't like her, either."

"Does anyone?"

"Hard to say. I suppose she can be charming."

"Charming as a snake."

That she sounded a bit indignant egged Chase on. "And she is an eyeful."

"An eyesore, you mean."

"Kathleen McKenna Farrell—is that the way your mother taught you to talk?"

She crossed her arms over her chest and lifted her chin. "My mother is a bit naive about people."

"I don't remember that about her. I only remember her being warm and kind and supportive," he said sincerely. "I figured you were the luckiest kid in the world to have her."

That took the wind out of Kate's sails. Even she couldn't argue with his complimenting her own mother. She wandered into the stand of tall pine, circling one tree, then another.

"We're getting away from the subject," she said. Her expression grew serious. "Chase, I know something's not right here." She took a deep breath and asked, "What's really going on with the refuge?"

Chapter Five

Chase should have known that Kate wouldn't be any
more shortsighted than she'd been as a kid when she'd
seen through his bravado to the hurt within. He'd appreciated that about her. That, and maybe a hundred
other things. All the more reason to feel guilty about
what he'd done to her.

He'd tricked her...used her...and then he'd up and
disappeared.

"I wish I knew what's going on," he admitted.
"Since the tourist season started, we've been cursed by
bad luck."

Kate nodded. "Doc's death. The downed fence.
Now the missing horses."

She didn't know the half of it. But she would before long, so Chase figured he might as well get what
had been eating at him off his chest.

"Before that, the tourist-mobile broke down. Not
that the old pickup didn't need a lot of work in gen-
eral. But it ran out of oil when it shouldn't have, and
no warning light ever came on. We put it to a faulty
wire and had to replace the engine."

"Ouch!"

"Damn straight, ouch. That could have been a mortgage payment," he said, still disgusted at the waste of money. "Then some workhorses got sick on fouled hay. Luckily Doc spotted the problem right away like he did with that weird virus. But no one caught the fire that torched one of the buildings Nathan was working on. We were damn lucky that it rained before the fire spread."

Her forehead furrowed. "You don't think..."

"That someone wants to drive the refuge out of existence?" Bone-tired, Chase set his shoulder against a tree and wondered if he would ever catch his breath. "I've been trying *not* to think that, but putting everything to coincidence is getting mighty hard."

Kate rested her back against the big old pine tree opposite him and hitched the heel of her red boot against its trunk. He could see the wheels of her mind clicking in the subtle change of her eyes. He'd once been familiar with her every expression, her every mood. He'd carried those impressions away with him and suspected that at least some of them would have a place in his memory forever.

But when she suddenly asked, "Why is Thea willing to pay above market for the land?" he realized she was still able to surprise him.

"Because she wants to make money on it."

"The question is how?"

"She's a real-estate developer, remember."

"That's what she said," Kate agreed. "But, like you, I wonder if the explanation is really that simple."

The reason he'd challenged Thea about wanting refuge land specifically.

"I don't know. But then, I don't know much lately."

He understood the Thea Lockridges of the world only on a surface level. Greed was greed no matter where a person hailed from. But he didn't have a clue what she might be planning beneath that beehive of hers.

Kate surprised him yet again when she asked, "Are you considering Thea's offer?"

"Why should I?"

"It is possible that her proposition might be the answer to the refuge's problems, isn't it?"

Anger swirled in the pit of his stomach. "Giving the mustangs less room to run free is a solution?"

"They're not running free now, Chase, not with fences and vetting, supplementary feed and round-ups," Kate argued. "Face it. You may be working in a less restrictive manner than normal, but you *are* managing the herd."

"Which is better than their giving up the will to live in feedlots where they can't run at all! They grow despondent. Many refuse to eat." He shook his head. "I've seen too many dead mustangs already."

"The reason you got involved in the first place?" She sighed. "Do you want to talk about it?"

"It's a long story, Kate."

"I'm not going anywhere."

Chase could almost hear her thousand and one questions. If he started, there would be no turning back. Did he want to open himself to her scrutiny? He had to admit that Kate deserved more than he'd given her so far. He couldn't make up for the past, but he could give her at least part of the truth.

Agitated, he shoved his hands in his pockets and began to pace. "When I left here, I hitched my way to Nevada, to my uncle Ross's spread."

"Peggy's brother?"

"Yeah."

Reminded of his gentle mother who'd died of abuse and neglect long before he'd hit puberty—before he was tall enough and strong enough to do something about his drunken no-good father—Chase nodded. He couldn't think of her without feeling sick inside.

"Ross was a good man," he said, continuing as much for himself as for Kate. "Tough, though. He took me in without any questions, but he worked my butt—both on the ranch and off—exactly like he did his own boys. He made sure I got my high-school diploma. And then he prodded me into taking courses that had to do with ranch management and animal husbandry at the local college. No degree," he added, just in case she was wondering.

Kate merely shrugged and said, "I know Nevada holds about half of our wild-horse population. And that the ranchers are fighting multipurpose usage of federal lands and want to restrict open range to their cattle."

"Some of them are hotheads, not averse to taking the law into their own hands and damn the consequences."

Chase stopped at the edge of a narrow ravine that zigzagged along the pine stand. He stared into the crevasse, unseeing, as he recalled the memory that drove him.

"One day I was out rounding up cattle with my cousins Lee and Mitch. I went after a few strays and by accident stumbled on a secluded water hole."

Though upwards of a dozen years had passed, the horror hadn't. "More than thirty mustangs had been shot to death." He glanced at Kate, whose expression reflected what he was feeling. "All they were doing was trying to get water to survive a while longer."

Her "How awful" sounded strangled.

Though he accepted the image that always followed him, Chase allowed himself to be distracted by a clump of flowers on the slope a few feet below. He stepped down and captured a bloom, delicate against his calloused hand, then approached Kate who seemed frozen to the spot.

He'd always thought the moments before twilight surrendered to dark were mystical. He could barely see her, bright red hair deepened to mahogany, eyes dark pools of pain, brimming with unshed tears.

Did she cry for the mustangs?

Or for him?

Not wanting to be pitied, he offered her the flower. "Venus slipper." When she didn't respond, he reached out to slide the orchid's stem behind her ear. She shuddered, and Chase thought she might bolt. "A beautiful bright spot in the dark," he murmured, trailing a fingertip along a curly wisp of hair that feathered her cheek. "Like you."

Her breath caught and she said softly, "I wish you hadn't seen that tragedy."

"Don't. I'm glad I did—I vowed never to forget. That season I started adopting mustangs."

"To protect them..."

"A drop in the bucket."

Unable to help himself, he ran his knuckles along Kate's jawline. He hadn't forgotten *her,* either. He hadn't even come close. He'd judged every woman he'd ever been with using her as a standard. Few had met her measure.

None had *been* her.

For months—since that Nash guy had divorced Kate and she'd moved back to Bitter Creek—he'd been tempted to seek her out. To learn if memory and reality had anything in common. But the past that goaded him had also stopped him. He'd been ashamed. And afraid.

And so he'd let it alone.

In the end she had come to him, even if the wild horses had been her excuse.

A sign?

He set a palm against the tree trunk above her head and leaned in. Her familiar scent teased him, her remembered warmth tormented him.

Staring into the face so close to his own, he recognized the curiosity in Kate's eyes. And the questions. She blinked but didn't glance away. She sighed but didn't speak. Her lips trembled. Parted. Fascinated by her lower lip, he ran his thumb pad along its fullness.

He remembered kissing this mouth. How could he forget?

He would have been less than a man if he didn't try to revive the past.

KATE'S EYES WIDENED when Chase's head dipped toward hers. As if from a distance—as if it was happening to someone else—she watched him move in on her in slow motion. She had the time she needed to duck away. She told herself to move, to get out of this while she could.

But curiosity held her fast, wouldn't let her budge. She tried to think. She couldn't. Like a deer caught in headlights, she was trapped, heart thundering, waiting for the inevitable.

And then it was too late to do anything but yield.

Kissing Chase was familiar and yet not. He was harder, stronger, more practiced than she remembered. She was older, wiser, more discerning. They weren't kids, doing what came naturally. They were adults, testing each other... testing themselves.

And then something changed.

Chase stopped holding back and kissed her like a man desperate for what he feared he couldn't claim. His muffled groan speared her with something Kate didn't want to feel. Confusing emotions engulfed her. Some small rational part of her thought to stop and push him away, but his urgency proved contagious.

Impulse wrapped her arms around his neck.

Memory fitted her mouth perfectly to his.

Need opened her to his invasion.

Running on instinct, she fed on the physical sensations swamping her as he moved in, pressing her back into the scratchy bark, tugging at her waist until her hips flowed forward, meeting his. Head light, body heavy, she gave herself up to the moment and a kiss so deep she couldn't stop the wanton sound that welled in her throat and escaped to his capture.

With a like groan, Chase slid his hand upward, finding the fullness of her breast. Blood rushing through her suddenly weak limbs, she nearly drowned in a wash of desire. She dug her fingers into his neck and shoulder and arched her back in an attempt to get even closer.

His mouth left hers with a gasp. He was having trouble breathing normally. As was she. Sucking air deep into her lungs, she willed her whirling head to clear. She hadn't been kissed so thoroughly since...

Since?

Maybe never.

Lingering emotions warred with good sense. Had Chase pressed the issue, she might have thrown herself back in his arms. But he seemed equally indecisive. And she began wondering what in the world had possessed her. How could she have lost her head so thoroughly?

She put her response down to madness—a full-moon night—and took control of the situation.

Palms levered against his chest encouraged Chase to back off. A few calming breaths, and her world began to right itself. The hour had grown late, their surroundings dark. She could barely make out his face. His thoughts were hidden from her. Good. That meant he couldn't read her confusion, either.

She tried to sound as if nothing had happened when she said, "Nathan and Merle are probably wondering if we fell into a sinkhole."

A low curse under his breath was followed by Chase's growling, "Then we'd better get back, hadn't we?"

As if part of some silent pact, neither said a word about the kiss as they climbed into the truck. Maybe Chase was regretting it already, Kate thought, wishing herself somewhere else. Anywhere but with him.

She pushed her thoughts away from Chase, tried to focus on other matters. As soon as they arrived at the refuge, she would make some excuse and leave for home. That would give her some breathing room.

And time to prepare for her night's adventure.

Kate reminded herself that she had a wild horse to find...and, if her instincts were correct, another truth to learn, as well.

ANNIE'S STOMACH turned itself inside out as she watched Chase and Kate Farrell alight from the Bronco and she was faced with the truth. Standing on the screened porch, she wasn't close enough to the parking area to hear what they were saying to each other, but between the full moon and the dim yard light, she certainly could read their body language. Both of them appeared tense. With each other.

A weight settled on Annie's chest and she could hardly think above the rushing noise filling her ears. She'd been dreading this. For once she'd hoped her instincts had been wrong, but no, they'd been on the money.

Something personal *was* going on between those two....

"Hey, is that Chase or what?" Nathan called irritably from the office. "If not, I'm gonna get outta here and find myself some grub."

Annie kept her voice sounding as natural as she could. "He's here."

Nathan and Merle had been waiting for Chase to show for the best part of an hour. Enough time for her to conjure all sorts of things going wrong.

Everyone else had left for home or town, including the volunteers who'd gone out with the employees. But the sisters had been around long enough for that gossipy Gerry to spill her guts about Kate's conversation with Nathan. The veterinarian had claimed she'd gotten into the mind of a horse and had seen a stampede, maybe the one that had killed Doc.

Annie wondered how many others Gerry had already told—not that she believed such spooky incidents had any real basis in fact.

But what if...

Wired, wanting to break up the cozy tête-à-tête between Chase and Kate that was making her sick, Annie was about to shout a greeting when the new vet abruptly waltzed over to her pickup. Chase stood staring after her for a minute before stalking toward the office.

Annie opened the screen door for him. "We were beginning to think you got lost."

Distracted, he muttered, "Something like that," and turned to watch the pickup shoot down the gravel road.

Swallowing her rising anger so he wouldn't notice was some trick. She took a deep breath and informed him, "Nathan and Merle have been waiting."

"Right."

He marched straight into the office without even looking at her. Right behind him, Annie cursed the day Kate Farrell had stepped her pretty red boots on the Bitter Creek Mustang Refuge.

"Did you find the missing horses?" Merle asked without preamble.

"No sign of them." Chase threw himself into a chair opposite his employees. "I guess that means that neither of you had any luck, either."

Nathan shrugged. "No one admits to seeing any stray mustangs."

"But you think they might have?"

"Someone must've. Those horses couldn't have up and disappeared into thin air."

"Not a hundred head," Merle agreed. "And not when they carry those freeze marks identifying them as being under BLM protection."

Needing Chase's attention, Annie placed a comforting hand on his shoulder and added, "Sounds like someone's making trouble for us on purpose."

"That's exactly what I'm afraid of."

And when the trouble had started, Chase had turned to *her* to talk things through, Annie remembered. And when he'd really been down, they'd even shared a couple of dinners. Finally. Progress! His wanting to confide in her had made everything she'd done for him worthwhile.

Though she'd always loved horses—the reason she'd visited the sanctuary in the first place—she hadn't sacrificed her real life just to help the mustangs. Her sights had been set on bigger game. Chase himself. She'd fallen in love with the man the moment she'd met him, had figured it was merely a matter of time and opportunity before he realized she was the woman he needed as his life's partner. And she'd been very clever on how to go about getting him.

With each problem that had crept up on the refuge, she'd offered Chase her sympathy and had volunteered her help in finding solutions. They'd grown closer—and would have grown intimate, she was certain—if only Kate Farrell hadn't appeared to upset things. The night before, Chase had even canceled the dinner she'd spent so much time planning and looking forward to. Even her reminding him about the welfare of the mustangs hadn't changed his mind.

Two damn days—and before that, months of gain—gone to dust.

"So what are we gonna do?" Nathan was asking.

"At the moment," Chase said grimly, "all we *can* do is keep our ears and eyes open for the trouble-maker."

But how did he figure he could manage that when all his spare attention seemed to be focused on the redhead? Annie wondered.

When she'd decided to go after Chase with everything she had, Kate Farrell was an obstacle she hadn't even considered. But she couldn't let a little unexpected deterrent discourage her, not after all her hard work. Never one to sit around and twiddle her thumbs while waiting for someone else to solve her problems, she wasn't about to start now. She wasn't about to let another woman seduce the man she loved without putting up a fight.

No matter that the vet seemed like a decent sort, Annie knew she had to act fast and not worry about scruples.

Where Chase Brody was concerned, she couldn't afford to have a conscience.

"STAY," KATE TOLD Wrangler, giving him the hand signal Doc had trained him to recognize. "I shouldn't be gone too long, so you wait for me here, okay?"

The patchwork mutt yawned loudly, turned in a full circle and plunked down on the old chair pillow she'd thrown in the bed of her pickup for him.

"Good boy."

Normally she wouldn't have brought a dog onto refuge land lest he inadvertently scare the horses, but Wrangler was a quiet guy and exceedingly well behaved. Doc had seen to that. While his slight size wouldn't afford much in the way of protection, she'd felt better having his company on the ride out. And

Doc had told her a body couldn't ask for a better watchdog. Not altogether comfortable wandering around the refuge by herself in the dark, she wouldn't mind Wrangler's guarding her back, even though from a distance.

If only Chase had believed her—or if Nathan hadn't warned her off seeking out the horses again—she wouldn't have considered coming out alone.

Kate started down the incline where she and Chase had found Sage and her band grazing. Since the horses had hung around the area for several days after the stampede, she didn't feature them drifting too far off now because of a minor scare.

Making her way by the glow of the full moon high in the sky—dawn was barely a few hours away—she checked the light hanging from her belt, using her free hand to shelter the high beam. She meant to use the bright light only as necessary. The less intrusive she was, the more likely she would be to get close to Chase's horses.

Chase.

She couldn't stop thinking about the man he'd become and the life he'd chosen for himself.

At first she'd been baffled by his apparent selflessness in taking on a burden the size of the refuge, but having had time to consider their earlier conversation, she thought she understood why. Chase had felt completely helpless upon finding those horses shot dead at their water hole.

Undoubtedly as helpless as he'd felt against his father when Vernon Brody had raised his hand to his wife.

Not that Peggy had been murdered.

Vernon had merely intimidated the sweet woman into staying away from doctors, who might have questioned or even reported her too-frequent scrapes and bruises. By the time she'd been desperately sick enough to defy her husband, the cancer had been unstoppable.

Despite the many years that had passed, Kate still remembered the night Chase had poured out his heart to her. His unresolved frustration. His grief. His guilt. Things he said he'd never shared with anyone else.

The correlation was clear to her. The wild horses were as helpless against men with high-powered rifles as Peggy had been against her husband's fists. She figured that, whether or not Chase consciously knew it, he was trying to atone for his inability to save his mother by defending other creatures who couldn't protect themselves.

And now a sizable part of his herd had disappeared.

He must be going nuts.

At the foot of the ravine Kate stood still and listened for equine sounds. The wind soughed around her and she imagined she heard a sharp bark. Wrangler? Or a coyote? The sound wasn't repeated, so she picked her way along the bank of the stream in the direction the mustangs had fled, careful to keep her boots dry. She flicked on her flashlight where the ravine took a sharp turn.

Stopping at the curve's end, she whistled softly, the combination of notes the same as she'd used that afternoon. Rather than proceeding forward, she waited. Whistled. Waited. Whistled and waited some more.

Ears attuned to the night, she picked out a faint snort and the clack of hooves against limestone. A second later a rock came clattering down the ravine behind her as if it had been kicked. Though she threw a nervous glance over her shoulder, she didn't really expect to see anything. The horses banded together, and she knew they were stealing toward her from the opposite direction.

A gust of wind curled around her body, bringing with it other noises that had nothing to do with horses.

The wind.

What an idiot! Feeling silly, she relaxed and whistled again.

Her reward came in some answering snorts. More clacks. A soft whinny.

She discerned the mustangs' approach even before she saw them. Spread along the side of the ravine, they advanced in fits and starts. She knew they'd recognized her whistle and in some respect trusted her or they wouldn't have responded. She stared in their direction until her eyes adjusted and she could make out not only their pale markings, but the shapes of even the darkest mares.

A single nervous neigh and some quick-hoofed dancing on rock made her stop and hold her breath. She glanced around. Of course she was alone. But the wind was still gusting and they must have caught her scent. She'd purposely worn Doc's vest so the horses would not only smell her, but him, as well. She'd hoped to put them at ease with his familiar presence.

The mares continued to move in her direction, and if she was mistaken, with less hesitation. Relieved— her plan seemed to be working—she let go of her held breath and pursed her lips to repeat the familiar notes.

Within moments the girls were surrounding her, near enough to take treats from one hand while letting her touch them with the other. Kate slowly made her way through the small band, all the while edging closer to Sage, who stood tense and aloof from the others.

The breeze sprang up and the lead mare's nostrils quivered. Sage made a noise that sounded distinctly like horse-grumbling. Kate's pulse threaded unevenly as the grulla picked her way closer, leading with her twitching nose. Doc's scent apparently confused her. Sage cocked her head, eyeing Kate suspiciously.

"You remember Doc, don't you, girl? He was your friend," she murmured, holding out a chunk of carrot to lure the horse closer. "Mine, too."

This time Sage ignored the treat in her hand and went straight for the vest, burying her nose in the folds of the well-worn cotton and snorting loudly. Pleased, Kate ran her hand along the left side of Sage's neck beneath the shaggy mane, her fingertips finding the freeze mark that was the mare's government identification number.

Senses fine-tuned, Kate heard a sharp if distant bark, but was too enthralled with her success to worry about it. Warm horseflesh quaked against her palm. The mare seemed caught up in snuffling Doc's scent and making low noises in the back of her throat.

Giving Kate the distinct impression that Sage was mourning him.

Concentrating on what she'd seen of the stampede the last time, she closed her eyes and opened her mind. Other distorted impressions immediately filled the void...

...*a sharp whine followed by horses bolting in every direction... thick white foam lathering a straining neck... wild eyes rolling...*

Kate's heart began to pump as rapidly as if she were part of the band. Again fear taunted her, but this time, not wanting to break her connection to Sage, she refused to let the emotion overwhelm her, not even when she heard the scream...

...human and yet not, the sound reverberated through her skull...struck terror in her heart... suddenly the sky was charged with sheet lightning and tilted crazily...another whine...a dog barking... muscular bodies pushing at her from both sides and behind...she couldn't move...nowhere to go...

Sage threw up her head, momentarily breaking the connection. Kate whispered calming words, all the while stroking the mare's short thick neck with both hands.

"We can't stop now, Sage," she whispered, sounds eerily echoing through her head. *Horses screaming. Dog barking.* "Not until I see everything. We can't stop," she repeated. "Not yet."

Not yet...

...sharp pain shot through her legs...a lurch forward...the sky breaking into a million shards... distorted images, closer...a lathered bay...a freeze mark across a paint's hindquarters...a dun dodging something below...human legs...boots suddenly dancing into air...

"Omigod!" Kate cried softly, tears squeezing through closed lids. "Doc!"

Through Sage's haunting memory, she became witness to the stampede that had killed her mentor. The images were unlike anything that any human could have seen, however, for the horse's vision was not binocular. She was seeing two different views—one from each eye—simultaneously.

The effect was confusing, dizzying.

She forced herself to hang on a moment longer...

... *dodging ... weaving ... circling ... escaping into a thick, wet emptiness ...*

But not before she saw something that didn't compute.

Heart pounding against her ribs, Kate flashed open her eyes, the misplaced image burned clearly into her. Realizing she'd stopped breathing, she gasped. Air exploded into her lungs and through her head, drowning out a sharp bark.

She'd been prepared to see Doc's death, but not this.

Not proof that his death had been no accident!

Chapter Six

Stunned, Kate barely registered the click that cut through the night. Sage's ears pricked and she snorted.

A high-pitched whine, closer, made *her* start.

What the hell was that?

Tension spread through the small band. All facing the direction from which she'd come, the mares were on alert—nostrils quivering, ears twitching, hooves dancing. Kate flashed a quick look around the ravine but didn't see or hear anything out of place. With senses far more finely tuned than hers, however, the mares were on edge, muscles bunched, as if waiting for Sage's signal to flee.

Another high-pitched whine and the grulla reared onto her hind legs, screaming her displeasure.

And an astonished Kate put a name to the sound.

A gunshot!

Instinct drove Kate toward cover, even as the wild horses exploded around her. Panicked, they bolted with her, and for a moment she thought she might be forced down under their hooves. But as if some otherworldly force protected her, she remained untouched.

Dodging behind a boulder as the last of the mares darted past, she huddled against the cool rock and tried to make sense of what was happening. Why would someone be shooting at the horses?

Or was *she* the target?

Either way, she couldn't chance a noise or movement that might alert the gunman. She hunched into a ball and huddled against the boulder. The heat of fear seared her, sending rivulets of sweat rolling down her spine and between her breasts. She'd never been in a situation like this before.

What to do?

How could she protect herself?

Confusion filled her when minutes passed and she heard nothing more threatening than the wind. Had she imagined the gunshots, then? Maybe no one was waiting for her with a loaded rifle, after all. Maybe she was just freaking out. Connecting with Sage had been such a powerful phenomenon . . . how could she be certain the gunshots hadn't been nothing more than echoes of the experience, rather than the whine of bullets speeding past her ear?

As much as she wanted to believe that, she couldn't. A very real threat had panicked those horses.

But a threat to whom? she wondered again.

Her mouth was dry, but her pulse had steadied. Uncoiling a bit, she strained to hear. Something. Anything.

Nothing.

No cocked rifle. No bullet whine. No skidding rock. Absolutely nothing to alarm her.

Was she safe, then? Or would leaving her hiding place make her the perfect target?

How much longer did she need to wait?

Suddenly something or someone scrabbling and slipping along pebbled rocks raised the hairs at the nape of her neck. Muscles bunched, Kate readied herself to run when a sharp bark made her pause. More barks.

Familiar barks.

Before she could fly to her feet, a furry body leapt over the boulder and lunged at her.

"Wrangler," she gasped in relief. Landing on her chest, he licked her face, wriggling as if he was trying to get inside her skin. Never so glad to see anyone, she hugged the mutt and ruffled his fur. "Let's get back to the pickup and head for home."

But she'd barely moved from her shelter when she heard the clop-clop of hooves. She froze and pinpointed the sound. Her blood ran cold.

It was metal hitting rock. A shoed horse.

The gunman!

Blindly she flew in the other direction, yelling, "Wrangler, c'mon!"

"Kate!"

Panicked, she didn't so much as pause at the sound of her name. She ran as fast as her legs would move, Wrangler alongside her, running and jumping and yapping as though they were playing a game.

"Kate, wait up!"

Hooves pounded the earth directly behind her as she clambered up the side of the ravine, Wrangler beating her to the flat above. He barked as if to spur her on, but she was tiring fast, could hardly catch her breath. The rider was gaining. She forced her legs to keep moving, even when she felt the horse's breath cross the back of her neck.

Sensing the rider dipping toward her, she yelled, "No-o-o!"

A band of steel hooked her waist and lifted her off her feet. She screamed and kicked out, her booted toe meeting his shin. A low male curse inspired her to more damage. Hand balled, she flashed out blindly, her fist meeting her attacker's middle.

With an "Oof" he dropped her.

Exhausted, winded, she sought the energy to get to her feet. But all she could do was lay there panting, staring up at the figure silhouetted by the moon.

Chase. Rifle in hand.

"WHAT THE HELL is wrong with you?" Chase yelled.

He was seeing-red angry, not because Kate had socked him, but because she was out here alone in the middle of the night. This was the kind of crazy stunt he would have expected of her when she was a kid. Obviously she had never completely lost her wild streak.

"Me?" she gasped. "I'm not the one holding the weapon."

Realizing his rifle was aimed at her, Chase lowered it to a nonthreatening position. "Satisfied?"

"Not by a long shot." A strangled giggle turned into a hiccup. "Stay away from me."

Wrangler barked and half-ran, half-slid down to Kate's side, where he sat, tongue lolling.

"Are you crazy?" Chase asked, more ticked off by the minute over her furtive excursion and those shots he'd heard. "Didn't you think you might get hurt out here?"

"Do you always shoot first, ask questions later?"

Chase went very still. Surely Kate couldn't believe he'd tried to shoot her. What would make her think he wanted to harm her in any way? Admittedly he'd thought about throttling her for coming out here alone at night—and the temptation was growing stronger.

Stiffly he informed her, ''My rifle hasn't been fired.''

''Right.''

She *didn't* trust him. Clenching his jaw, he tossed the rifle down to her. ''Your imagination's on overload. Check for yourself.''

Kate felt the barrel, smelled the chamber, then looked up at him in astonishment. ''It wasn't you.'' She scrambled to her feet and handed the weapon back to him. ''Someone did shoot at me, honest. At least twice.''

''I heard three shots,'' he admitted.

That *someone* had discharged a weapon wasn't in dispute. Once more Chase glared into the dark as if he could pick out the perpetrator. But whoever had released a couple of loads in her direction was undoubtedly long gone. He secured the rifle to his saddle and held out his arm to her.

''Take my hand.'' He removed his foot from a stirrup. ''And get up behind me.'' When she hesitated, he said, ''Deadwood doesn't bite.'' Though *he* might be tempted.

For a moment Chase thought Kate would balk at the order, but apparently she was more concerned about being alone on foot than about sacrificing her autonomy. She slipped her hand into his, stuck her boot in the stirrup and bounced upward, swinging her free leg over Deadwood's rump.

Her settling in behind him reminded Chase of a night they'd ridden out into the wilderness together many years ago.

A night it shamed him to remember.

Wondering if Kate could possibly know the whole truth, he felt his anger slip away. And even if she'd remained in the dark all these years, she still had good reason to distrust him. Clucking, he moved his horse back along the ravine the way he'd come. Wrangler scampered alongside them, every so often racing ahead and waiting for them to catch up.

"So what were you doing out here?" he asked, though he figured he already knew.

"What are you doing out here *on a horse?*" she countered. "You told me the mustangs would be scared off by anyone who was mounted."

"I wasn't here to check on the mustangs."

"Then what?"

"I couldn't sleep," he hedged. Strictly speaking, he wasn't lying. Thinking about how he'd planned to spend the wee hours before dawn had kept him awake until it was time to leave. "What about you?"

"Neither could I."

Chase didn't believe her for a moment. The questions could wait, he decided, not unaware of Kate's trembling against him despite her argumentative attitude. How could he miss it when she was pressed so close that a sheet of paper wouldn't fit between them? He shifted in the saddle, trying to find some zone of comfort.

Taking an unauthorized tour of Lockridge Acres would have to wait. He really should throttle Kate for screwing up his plans. Now, if she knew the whereabouts of his horses, Thea Lockridge had another day to cover.

When they reached the pickup, Wrangler jumped into the back and watched as Chase helped Kate down, then quickly dismounted. Not unaware of the way she was eyeing him distrustfully, Chase tied Deadwood's reins to a metal loop on the truck.

"I'm all right now," she said.

"Good."

"Then what are you planning on doing?"

"Driving."

"*My* pickup?"

"I don't see any other vehicles." He grabbed his rifle and slid behind the wheel. "What are you waiting for?"

Without further argument, Kate climbed in beside him. Chase figured she was more shaken up than she wanted to admit. She'd always had bravado—one of the many things he'd admired about her when they were younger. But whatever was going on at the refuge was serious business.

And a little misplaced bravado could get Kate killed.

GOING OVER AND OVER what she'd seen when her mind had merged with Sage's, Kate kept her peace until Chase stopped the pickup and cut the engine. Startled back to reality, she felt disoriented. She'd been too preoccupied to pay attention to their route, although she had noticed how uncharacteristically slowly Chase had been driving in deference to his horse. She glanced out the passenger window at a solitary log cabin she'd never seen before.

"Where are we?"

Chase was already leaving the cab, her key ring in hand, when he said, "Home."

His home, of course, not hers.

Not that she was in any big hurry to drive back to town alone—she was still spooked and rightly so—Kate decided that not letting Chase boss her around was a matter of principle. She flew out the door, catching up to him before he reached his horse. She grabbed his arm to make him pay attention.

"My keys?"

He slid them into his pocket. "Later."

"Now."

Her mouth went dry with the challenge, which Chase was ignoring. She could feel his stare from beneath his hat brim. Her pulse picked up a beat. The flesh beneath her fingers burned as something other than animosity flared between them. She let go of his arm as fast as she would a hot poker, the kiss that never should have happened clear in her mind.

Why couldn't she just be immune to him? Kate wondered. What hold could he possibly have over her after all these years? After the way he'd broken her heart?

Chase was the first to move away. He untied Deadwood from the gate. Pulse steadying, Kate watched him lead the dark gelding to a large corral that held two other dozing horses. In record time, he stripped off his mount's saddle and bridle. After checking the horse over to make certain he'd cooled down, Chase turned him out.

And before he could catch her watching him, Kate spun around to pay some attention to the dog, who'd quietly moved across the truck's bed to be closer to her. She ruffled Wrangler's fur, then pulled a smelly tidbit from one of her vest pockets.

"Do you believe that man's nerve, keeping us here against our will?" As the dog eagerly took the treat from her hand and crunched away, she said, "Thanks for coming to my rescue, roomie."

"What about me?" Chase was directly behind her, his warm breath fanning her exposed neck. "Don't I deserve your thanks, too?"

Quick as a flash, she spun around, at the same time palming another liver-flavored biscuit. "Right. Thanks." She offered him the dog treat.

Again his expression was shadowed when he said dryly, "I'll pass," and walked right on by her. Fetching his rifle from the cabin, he headed for the house.

Kate felt awful. He really had come to her rescue, and how had she repaid him? First she'd accused him of using her for target practice. And then she'd responded by mocking him. Truth to tell, she wasn't in a playful mood. She was still spooked, and joking around was her way of working out the stress.

Signaling Wrangler to come with her, she followed Chase, but couldn't quite work up an apology. Instead, she asked, "So when do I get my keys back? I'd like to get some sleep, if you don't mind."

"My couch isn't too lumpy. Or you could join me in bed."

His turn to mock her.

"My turn to pass."

The front door was open. Chase flipped a switch and two pottery-based table lamps came on, spreading a soft golden glow over the interior. While sparsely furnished, the large combination living area/kitchen was inviting. Pine cabinets and furniture, couch with colorful Western-print cushions, creatively framed photographs of mustangs on the walls. So that Chase couldn't get too disturbingly close to her, she chose the solitary leather chair.

Sinking into the seat that was nearly big enough for two of her, she asked, "Now what?" as Wrangler settled at her feet.

Chase set his rifle on his gun rack, then hung his hat and jacket on pegs next to the door. "Now suppose you do some talking. What was going on in that ravine?"

She'd figured he'd get around to interrogating her. And she wanted to talk about Doc's death. But where to start? If she told him she'd had another vision, the joke might be on her... and yet how could she keep what she'd seen to herself merely because he was a skeptic?

Chancing Chase's derision, Kate said, "The stampede that killed Doc was no accident." And eyed him carefully for his reaction.

He sat on the couch arm. "Go on." His features were void of any judgment.

"Sage and I shared a few thoughts tonight." Tension mounting, she turned inward, replayed the memory. "It started like the last time... the wild horses running scared... then I realized I wasn't part of the stampede but separate from it."

Still expressionless, he asked, "How do you mean?"

"I saw as if from a distance," she explained, another image clarifying. She took a big breath. "I saw *him*... Doc. I—I think he was already dead." Her stomach turned as she remembered sharp hooves trampling the body, boots dancing in the air. "The thing was...Sage and her band were still in the corral. The horses I saw...their identification...the BLM freeze marks ran across their hindquarters.''

''While the horses in Sage's band are all ID'd across their necks,'' Chase said slowly.

''Exactly.'' Heart beginning to hammer as it had earlier, she went on. ''Sage was going nuts. The other mares were pushing and shoving. I flew...'' She caught herself before saying something foolish. ''I mean, Sage flew upward and crashed her hooves into the fence boards. I guess the others did, too. Then suddenly they were free...headed away from the stampede—but not before I saw it.''

''Saw what?''

Kate took a deep breath and conjured the memory that had stunned her. ''A stirrup...a boot...a person's leg.'' She stared directly at Chase when she said, ''The storm didn't spook those horses. Something very human did.''

He didn't react.

Disappointed, Kate told herself she shouldn't have bothered. Obviously he didn't believe her. But who else could she have told? That the sheriff would buy her story was even more unlikely. Perhaps Nathan Lantero was the only one she could trust to understand.

And so Chase's unexpected ''Did you see the person?'' made her catch her breath.

''What?''

''The person who started the stampede?''

''You believe me?''

''I have reason to believe Doc's death was no accident myself,'' he said, rising from the couch arm. ''Did you see the person's face?''

Her frustration dissolving, she shook her head. "Everything was happening so fast."

"But you're certain you saw a mounted rider?"

"Positive. Chase, I don't have an overactive imagination and I'm not crazy," Kate assured him. "I realize you have more than a few reservations, but—"

"I believe you." Chase stopped directly in front of her and stared, as if trying to read her mind. "At least part of me does."

"I suppose that's a start."

In truth, Kate was relieved that Chase was agreeable to being open, if nothing more. She knew he'd want to find the person responsible for starting the stampede that killed Doc as much as she did.

"Now the question is, who else believes you?" he asked, moving away.

"What do you mean?"

"Someone took more than one shot at you tonight."

"Or at the horses." Though she'd already considered the possibility that the gunman had been after her, Kate still didn't want to believe it.

"The horses make bigger targets. They're a damn sight harder to miss."

"Maybe the shooter missed on purpose, because he only meant to scare me off."

"But scare you off...*why?*"

Chase's implication about someone else's believing her became clear. If the person who'd started the stampede got wind of her intentions to learn more details...

Suddenly shaky inside, Kate said, "Other than you, the only person I talked to about what I saw this afternoon was Nathan."

"Then he knew you meant to try again."

She nodded. "He warned me off."

"Warned?"

"Not like that. He thought I should let it alone. I guess he figured I was obsessing over Doc's death. At that point, I didn't think the stampede was anything other than a terrible freak accident. And I'm certain Nathan was just trying to be a friend."

Appearing troubled, Chase said, "And you didn't say a word to anyone else?"

"I didn't, but I suppose Nathan could have... or that volunteer who was working with him. I'm pretty sure she overheard." She remembered the young woman's avid expression. "Most folks around here wouldn't take the story seriously. They'd say I was delusional or something."

Unfortunately she was used to a condescending attitude from the citizens of Bitter Creek. Even those who were satisfied with her veterinary services made a joke of her so-called gift, often to her face.

"But a smart miscreant wouldn't leave anything to chance," Chase insisted.

Making Kate squirm. "And what if no one was after me specifically? The person who's been messing with the refuge could have been up to some new dirty deed and didn't expect to run into company."

"You've got a point," he conceded.

Though he didn't sound convinced. He was pacing as though the continuous movement helped him think.

"What about you?" Kate asked. "You never did say how you found me."

"I already told you I was out riding because I couldn't sleep."

Chase avoided looking at her directly, making Kate think he was telling only a half-truth. Since Lockridge Acres adjoined that part of the refuge, the spread immediately came to mind. But if he planned to check Thea's property for himself, why didn't he just admit as much?

"I heard a shot," Chase was saying. "I was already heading in that direction to investigate when Wrangler started to bark. I found him in the bed of your pickup. He was anxious as hell to get out of there. I didn't figure you were the one doing the shooting, so I told him to fetch you and I followed."

As if he knew the humans were talking about him, Wrangler sat up and yawned. Kate scratched the dog's head, muttering, "Fetch me, huh? And you're not convinced that *I* can talk to animals."

"I never said animals couldn't understand certain commands. But I also never said I could see inside the mutt's head." He was towering over her, his face pulled into a scowl. "And don't try to make light of the situation, Kate. You could have gotten yourself killed."

"As if you would care."

"You really do think I'm heartless."

Even as she said, "You'd have to give me reason to think otherwise," Kate knew she was being unfair.

A man without a heart wouldn't be trying to protect a herd of mustangs that many ranchers across the Western states thought of as worthless pests who ruined the range for their cattle. But she refused to take the words back. He *had* been heartless to her, years ago, when he'd left town without a word. And even now he didn't seem inclined to offer any explanations. Thinking about it made her angry all over again.

And so when Chase ordered, "Don't pull another stunt like that," he raised her hackles.

"Excuse me? You're not *my* boss."

"This land is under my management!"

Popping out of the chair, Kate was practically nose to chin with Chase. He didn't give her breathing room, so she shoved by him, silently cursing when the brief contact made the breath catch in her throat. His following on her heels agitated her further.

But she stood her ground. "So you're going to *what* if I don't agree? Ban me from the refuge? Turn down vet services you'll undoubtedly need?"

His complexion ruddy, he said, "Don't make more of this than I meant."

"What did you mean?"

"To keep you from being mounted on a wall like one of Thea's trophies."

The image clear in her mind, Kate shuddered. And cooled down a bit. The reference to Thea cinched her Lockridge Acres theory. And he did seem as though he cared what happened to her. Or what would happen to the refuge if there was another tragic accident, a cynical little voice in her head countered.

Once more, his not-so-subtle insinuation struck her. "Wait a minute. You're making whoever's been messing with the refuge out to be a murderer."

"Isn't that what we've just been talking about?"

Chase had said he had reason to believe Doc's death was no accident....

"Whoa. I hadn't exactly gone there yet. I was thinking more in terms of someone running the horses off the property and Doc's being unfortunate enough to get in the way."

"He probably was in the wrong place at the wrong time," Chase agreed. "But if he recognized the rider and figured things out . . ."

She shook her head. "Killing a man over some rustled horses—that doesn't add up in my book."

"You're still the innocent, aren't you? You don't expect the worst of people because you don't have it in you to think that way." Chase sounded truly amazed.

Kate's mouth gaped open. *Innocent? Still?* If she didn't know better, she would think he was referring to her getting involved with him in the first place.

"So I don't know what to think." She took a big breath. "Murder . . . I guess we should alert the sheriff."

"And tell him Sage showed you Doc's death?"

"What, then?"

"We figure out who. Find a way to prove it."

"I'm too tired to play detective right now," Kate protested, exhaustion making every bone in her body feel heavy as lead. Too much new information was assaulting her, and she needed some time to assimilate it all. "I need sleep."

"Figuring things out can wait until tomorrow." He indicated a spot behind her. "My bedroom's right through that door."

Not planning to join him, she muttered, "Don't start," even as her imagination set to work.

Her in his bed . . . his body curled around hers . . . heat throbbing through every limb . . .

"I was planning on taking the couch," he said, dashing the fantasy before it had time to expand.

Her turn to look away from him. "Does the door have a lock?"

"You're safe from me."

Her insides fluttered. She wasn't any safer from Chase Brody than she'd been all those years ago. That was clear to her. Since he didn't give her a direct answer about the door, she checked for herself. The bolt worked fine. The only problem was, *she'd* be able to undo it....

Remembering the two ranches she needed to visit the next day, she got a grip on herself. "I have a long day ahead of me. Do you have a problem getting up with the sun?"

Chase checked his watch. "In an hour and a half? No, no problem. Sleep is such a luxury, anyway."

She didn't miss the irony. If he'd appeared tired to her earlier, he now looked as exhausted as she felt. Compassion for him warred with her good sense, and in the end, she said, "Make that three and a half hours," and whistled for the dog.

Wrangler trotted straight into Chase's bedroom and Kate closed the door behind him.

Running on empty wouldn't do either of them any good, especially not if they expected to identify a murderer.

CHASE WAITED until he heard Kate slide the bolt into place before locking the entry door and removing the rifle from its rack. Turning off the lights, he stretched out on the couch, setting the weapon alongside him on the floor.

Not that he believed they were in for a direct attack. Sneaking around and taking potshots from behind a rock seemed more like the villain's style.

But, just in case...

Sleep called his name, but when Chase closed his eyes, Kate danced behind his lids. Not the adult Kate, but the girl he'd abandoned. She'd never stopped haunting him. Ironic. He'd always liked his employer's daughter—she'd never judged him—but when he'd begun wooing her, it hadn't been his idea.

He and the Duran brothers had all been drunk the night they'd made the wager. Someone had called him "trailer trash" to his face, and he'd been spoiling for a fight. Buck and Gil had dragged him off, told him to accept who he was. Determined to prove them wrong—all of them, including his so-called friends—he'd bragged that he'd have it all someday.

A nice girl on his arm. A great place to live. Money lining his pockets.

Gil had been the one to suggest he put his money where his mouth was. The three of them had been working on the Farrell Ranch, Gil full-time and Buck and him after school and on the weekends. They all knew Kate Farrell. Gil said that if he could seduce her by the time he and Buck graduated, he'd prove them wrong and win the bet. Then he'd have both the nice girl and the money.

Knowing fifteen-year-old Kate was a little sweet on him, anyhow, Chase hadn't thought twice before accepting the wager. Nor had he thought about Kate's feelings if she ever learned why he'd spent months courting her under her parents' worried eyes. He'd enjoyed her company, had watched her bloom as she'd fallen in love with him.

But even after their one night together, he hadn't consciously realized how much Kate meant to him.

That she'd been a virgin was expected, and yet his taking that from her on a bet had shamed him. The next morning he'd been in a rotten mood as he and the Duran brothers worked, putting in fence posts. So when Gil pulled out the whiskey bottle at lunch, Chase had indulged to dull the pain.

Chase stared into the dark, remembering how he'd vowed never to tell his friends he'd succeeded in seducing Kate.

He'd decided to break it off with her, concede the bet and pay up. He hadn't cared about the money, but thinking about being without Kate in his life made him drink past his tolerance level.

What had happened after that had made him pledge never to take another drink.

And once he was on the road, he'd convinced himself he was acting in Kate's best interests by not contacting her, but underneath he'd known the truth: he was the coward she'd accused him of being. He hadn't had the guts to speak to her for fear he might spill out the truth.

He was still a coward, Chase thought, all hope of sleep gone. There was no explanation for his actions. No forgiveness. He wouldn't expect it of her, even as he hadn't expected his punishment to come so late and so sharp.

Though he'd been keeping himself from admitting as much, Chase knew he was in love with Kate Farrell, and he guessed he had been all along.

Chapter Seven

Remembering she'd promised Ellen Weber she would help sort through her father's things, Kate spent some time in Doc's study early the next evening, going through stacks of papers, throwing away travel brochures and junk mail.

So far that day, she'd ridden out to two ranches. One of the owners had some sick cows. The other was new in the area and needed to talk to her in depth before deciding whether or not he wanted a woman to vet his animals. It seemed he did. She'd returned to her office only to find a little girl waiting on the stoop, cradling a hurt cat in her arms. After which, she'd taken care of several routine visits. She'd even squeezed in a short but refreshing nap before showering and getting ready to meet Chase.

Anxious, she checked the time. Her watch informed her she still had an hour to kill before she was to leave for Rowdy's Bar and Gruel where she'd insisted he meet her to discuss who—other than Thea Lockridge—had reason to want the refuge annihilated. Chase had balked at coming into Bitter Creek, but she'd figured it was time he got over himself. She'd been adamant and he'd reluctantly given way. Though she'd won this round, she still wondered why.

Because he wanted her cooperation in solving the identity of the villain?

Or because he wanted *her*?

The speculation made Kate shift uncomfortably in her chair, especially because she no longer knew what *she* wanted.

To distract herself from speculating, she picked up Doc's current journal—he'd always kept notes about his patients over and above the professional files in the office. He not only wrote about their medical conditions, but added his thoughts. His intention, he'd told her once, was to write a book about his more interesting and humorous experiences with animals after he retired.

Another dream that had gone begging with his death.

Opening the leather-bound book to the last entry, she realized Doc had made a notation the day he'd died.

Need to check on Sage and her band. Still bamboozled about the source of the virus. With all the other things going on at the refuge, can't help but wonder if someone didn't let a sick horse loose...

So *Doc* had suspected. A creepy feeling stole through Kate.

All day she'd avoided thinking about the events of the night before, but with time to kill, she couldn't help it. What if Chase had been correct and the perpetrator had made sure Doc couldn't talk? What if the villain figured *she* knew too much? Kate took a deep breath and reminded herself that, while she'd been shot at, she hadn't been hurt. She held on to the possibility that the person's intent had been to scare her off, not kill her.

Wondering what other notes Doc had made about the situation, she paged backward, eventually coming to an entry about one of his more unusual patients. A human being. A volunteer on the refuge had been so startled by the stallion charging him in mock challenge, that he'd fallen over backward, managing to cut his hand on the fence.

A goofy accident, nothing serious. Cleaned and bandaged the wound and told the boy to stop wearing that perfume that aggravates the stallion so much.

Chuckling, Kate remembered Doc telling her that was how he'd gotten his nickname—by administering first aid to some of the townspeople and recommending treatment for simple illnesses over the years. Not that he'd ever overstepped his bounds by dispensing prescription medication or trying to take care of a serious condition. But Bitter Creek was a small town without a physician, and people were reluctant to make the drive to find one unless the situation truly called for it.

A knock at the door surprised her. Setting down the journal, she left the study, wondering if Chase had chosen to meet her here, rather than at the bar. Opening the door gave her another surprise.

"Annie."

"Hi. I was in town to buy groceries, and I decided to take a chance that you'd be in. I was hoping we could talk . . . if you're not too busy."

Dark hair swinging along her cheek, Annie peered into the living room as if making sure they were alone.

"I can spare a few minutes. Come on in." Kate led the volunteer around several boxes she'd brought from her old quarters but had not yet managed to unpack. "Sorry about the mess. I'm not even totally moved in yet. Can I get you something to drink?"

"No need."

Annie perched on the couch, and Kate took the threadbare chair that had been Doc's favorite.

"So what's up?"

"I need to talk to you about Chase," Annie said without preamble. "I'm worried sick about him."

Immediately on edge at the volunteer's possessive tone, Kate asked, "How so?"

"He's worn-out with hard work and terrible stress. I, uh, know about the problems he's been having at the refuge. He used to talk to me about them. But not lately and I don't understand why." Expression forlorn, Annie sighed. "All of a sudden he's keeping his concerns to himself, and I don't think that's good for him."

Considering her upcoming rendezvous with Chase, Kate squirmed inwardly. He was talking to *her* now, and she didn't think Annie would appreciate knowing that. Kate was getting the distinct impression that Annie and Chase had had something personal going until recently. So what had changed? Her walking back into his life?

She tried placating Annie. "He probably needs to think things through himself."

"He's been doing that ever since Doc's death—such a terrible accident."

Kate had to hold herself back from contradicting Annie. Until she and Chase had more to go on, they'd agreed to keep their suspicions to themselves. And she certainly didn't want whoever had been shooting at her to make a more serious effort to shut her up.

So all she said was, "Doc's death was terrible, all right."

"I guess you were pretty close to him."

"Since I was a kid. I became a vet because of Doc. He was my mentor."

"Sorry." Hardly taking a breath, Annie swiftly turned the conversation around. "As I was saying, Doc's death really affected Chase. And now those horses vanishing into thin air haven't helped things."

"He's not too happy," Kate agreed.

"Of course not." A strange glint in her normally soft blue eyes, Annie asked, "So what does he think is going on?"

Kate realized Annie was pumping her for information, as though she felt she had a stake in Chase and was afraid of being replaced. Kate wanted to tell the pretty volunteer she had nothing to worry about in the personal department, but the words wouldn't come.

"I guess you'd have to ask Chase what he's thinking, Annie. Though so many things have gone wrong lately, it would be difficult for anyone to believe it's all coincidence."

"There are some people around here who'd like to see the refuge fail."

"Like Thea Lockridge."

"Not just her. Other folks . . . including Nathan."

Startled, Kate asked, "What about Nathan?"

"He thinks the Lakota have a right to the land."

Something Kate hadn't realized. She wondered if Chase had. "He actually told you that?"

"Not anything about the refuge failing. But one day we were talking about the pictographs on the limestone bluffs. That's when Nathan said the land was sacred to his people and that they'd lost out on their chance to reclaim it."

Which made Kate wonder exactly how resentful Nathan Lantero might be. And if he felt so strongly about the issue, why would he have gone to work for Chase?

Unless being part of the refuge staff suited some dark purpose...

As a kid, Nathan hadn't been able to contain his jealousy of her because of the attention she received from Delbert. He'd found numerous ways to get even, though she had to admit he'd been pretty straightforward about his animosity. He'd never sneaked around behind her back, rather had always challenged her to her face. Besides which, she'd thought Nathan had gotten over his youthful insecurity and had reformed his ways.

But what if he hadn't?

What if he was getting even with Chase because of hard feelings over the land? Kate hated the thought, but she couldn't banish it.

"Have you told Chase what Nathan told you?"

The other woman's blue eyes went wide. "I wasn't implying that Nathan was guilty of anything! I just meant that not everyone thinks so much land being used to let some old mustangs run free is the right purpose. I personally can't see it being used for anything else."

And now that she'd done some exploring herself, had formed a tenuous bond with Sage's band, neither could Kate. "I understand you've volunteered to work on the refuge three summers in a row. That's very dedicated."

"After teaching remedial-reading to a bunch of unruly teenagers the rest of the year, coming out here is a breath of fresh air. I think of my time around the wild horses as a vacation for my soul."

The horses? Or Chase himself?

They talked for a few more minutes before Annie departed, leaving Kate wondering about her true purpose for dropping by in the first place. While she'd expressed an appropriate amount of concern about Chase in relation to the refuge, Annie hadn't made any suggestions about lifting his burden. Nor had she asked for counsel.

Leaving Kate with the distinct impression that Annie had been trying to feel her out to see what was going on between her and Chase.

If only she had an answer.

"WHAT IN THE WORLD got into Chase?" Buck mused. "He never comes into town."

"Unusual," Merle agreed, blowing cigarette smoke at him. "Maybe he's taken leave of his senses. Too much responsibility can do that to a person."

"Can't say I feel sorry for him," Buck muttered, turning his attention to his beer.

Neither did Merle.

Propped on a stool in Rowdy's Bar and Gruel, she glanced at the table across the room where Chase sat alone. After nodding to them when he'd entered a few minutes ago, he'd parked himself in the shadows. His hat rode low on his forehead as if he'd meant the wide brim to hide him from the other patrons. As usual, he was nursing a mug of coffee, instead of something more potent.

She remembered a long-ago time when he'd been fun and full of the devil. My, my, how life had changed him.

Then again, look what life had done to her.

Her insides clutching, Merle took a long drag on her cigarette and turned her attention away from Chase to a closer table where Thea Lockridge held court like some kind of queen bee. What a piece of work that bitch was—bringing her California money to Bitter Creek so she could ruin it for the people who'd lived here all their lives.

Three strangers accompanied the blonde, all city-slick men dressed like dime-store cowboys. No doubt they were searching for a piece of the authentic West, and Thea had brought them to Rowdy's for the atmosphere and greasy burgers. Smoke-filled, thin walls vibrating with a twangy country tune, decorated in Formica, vinyl and chrome, floors strewn with sawdust to absorb liquor spills and splatters off the grill, this dump was as authentic as it got.

Merle's gaze settled on the youngest of Thea's companions. The dark-haired man was of special interest to her, not because he was particularly good-looking, but because his well-muscled body made her thighs quake. She'd get to him eventually—anticipation was part of the fun. Meanwhile she'd enjoy admiring him from afar.

Buck's poking her in the arm disrupted her fantasies. "Uh-oh. Look who just walked in."

Merle spun around on her stool as Kate Farrell crossed to Chase's table. Without moving his butt off his chair, Chase indicated she should sit. The vet tossed her ponytail, plunked herself down and signaled the waitress. But their casual attitudes didn't fool her. The sparks between them were obvious to anyone with eyes to see.

Buck edged closer. "What do you think they're up to?"

So maybe Buck was a little dense. Shaking her head, Merle gave him a sideways look.

"Getting rid of some of that stress he's been under. Not that it'll do him any good in the long run. Chase is too spooked by all those horses up and disappearing to let it alone. I figure he means to find out what happened to them no matter what it takes."

"Good luck to him, then," Buck muttered. "For all he knows, the sky coulda opened up and they all rode straight into heaven."

Someday, Merle thought, the ground would open and issue Chase an invitation in the other direction.

Though she'd like to hide her feelings, she couldn't help but glare at him and Kate. Why should he have everything when she was left with nothing? His fault she was alone. His fault she turned out like her mother.

Deciding she didn't want to wait, after all, Merle crushed the remaining life out of her cigarette. "Listen, Buck, I'll catch you tomorrow."

"You going home?"

"Yep." Merle winked. "Eventually and not alone."

Opening another shirt button to reveal the hollow between her small breasts, waterfalling her newly washed silky hair over one shoulder, she sidled over to

Thea Lockridge's table. Standing slightly behind the blond beehive, she set a hand on her waist, stuck out her hip and stared at the dark-haired young man until he noticed her. Definitely appreciative.

"Hey, stranger, know how to Texas two-step?"

"No, ma'am," he said, rising, "but I been told I'm a fast learner." He took her elbow. "I'm Hank."

Merle smiled and glanced over at Chase's table. He and the vet seemed to be arguing about something. Maybe Chase wouldn't be relieving his stress tonight, after all.

But *she* would. Hank's coming home with her would make her feel a whole lot better. And while she and the dime-store cowboy were setting off the fires of passion, she'd imagine Chase beating off the fires of hell.

No more than he deserved for ruining her life.

WATCHING MERLE HEAD for the small dance floor with Thea's friend disgusted Chase. Bad enough she let the locals take advantage of her. But another land grabber? He'd like to have a serious talk with her, but he didn't think she'd appreciate advice on her love life from him.

The waitress broke into his thoughts, setting down a beer in front of Kate and refilling his coffee. "Your food'll be up in a minute, hon."

"Thanks, Ina." Kate sipped her beer and barely waited for the waitress to turn her back before saying, "About last night. You were riding to Lockridge Acres to look for the mustangs, weren't you?"

Startled by the accusation, he glowered at her. "Watch your mouth, woman."

"Excuse me?"

He shot a glance at Thea a few tables away, but she and her companions were intent on their conversation. "Keep your voice down. You want everyone to hear?"

Appearing smug, Kate said, "Then I was right. Are you going to try again? Tonight?"

Her questions were getting his back up. "Whatever I do is my business."

"I'm going with you."

His mouth got the better of him. He said, "And put yourself in possible danger," before realizing he'd confirmed her suspicions.

"Big deal. I don't even know if I'm safe in my own bed anymore."

"That's easily enough taken care of." He tried to rattle her. To make her think twice about going with him. "You don't have to sleep alone."

Kate narrowed her gaze when she said, "And I'm sure *you'll* be happy to volunteer."

"I was thinking of Wrangler. Good watchdog."

He was only half-serious about the dog, and if Kate's heightened color was any indication, she knew it. She tried to hide behind her beer mug.

The blush softened her, made her prettier, reminded him of the first time he'd kissed her. She'd blushed then, too. After which, she'd kissed him back. How the hell it was possible to remember was a mystery to him, but he recalled every detail as if the eighteen years that had passed since had been no more than eighteen days.

Chase resigned himself to taking Kate with him when he rode onto Lockridge Acres later that night. She had his number. And he had hers. She would be safer with him than following him, as he had no doubt she would. By involving her more directly, he could at least keep his eye on her, could protect her from running headlong into danger.

"All right. You can come with me. As long as I'm in charge. Agreed?"

He figured it irked her to say, "Agreed," rather than arguing the fine points. "Why?" she added.

Recognizing that suspicious narrowing of her eyes, he said, "Because I know how you felt about Doc."

He'd liked the old man, too. And considering Doc's death had something to do with him, Chase felt the need to learn who was responsible for that stampede. On the other hand, Kate's emotions were tied up in the situation. She'd loved the old man like a father, something Chase had trouble relating to. He hadn't had so much as a sorrowful thought when he'd heard his old man had died.

Kate shoved the past aside, saying, "We're getting off the subject."

"I didn't know we'd started."

"Now's as good a time as any. Let's start with Annie's unexpected visit a little while ago."

"Don't tell me you're suspicious of *her*. She has nothing at stake."

"But Nathan Lantero does."

"Nathan?"

"Annie said he told her the refuge was sacred to his people."

"I heard the Lakota wanted the land and that my deal with the governor didn't make them happy," Chase admitted, "but I didn't know Nathan felt one way or the other about it."

"Annie seemed to think he did, although she quickly assured me she didn't mean to imply that Nathan was guilty of anything."

"All the same, she came to see you to tell you about it."

"Uh, not exactly. We were talking about a different issue before we got onto the subject of who might be happy to see the sanctuary closed down."

Chase sensed she'd just skipped over something he should know about. He was tempted to worm the information out of her, but he was too tired to wear her down. He had to trust that, if it was important, Kate would tell him.

"Here you go, hon." Ina stood over them with two plates in hand. They moved their drinks and the waitress set down their burgers and fries. "Anything else I can get you? Another beer?"

Kate shook her head. "I'm fine."

"Nothing for me," Chase said, his juices flowing at the first whiff. Not used to having supper so late, he was extremely hungry. He took a big bite of his burger and washed it down with coffee.

"I'll leave the tab, then," the waitress said. "Holler when you're ready to pay. No rush."

Chase continued eating like the starving man he was. When the record on the jukebox ended, he glanced over at the dance floor. Merle had herself wrapped around the wannabe cowboy. Neither of them seemed to notice the lack of music. And when the next tune started up, a throaty-voiced woman wailing about a lost love, he looked away.

Picking at her food, Kate was staring at him, her hunger all in her eyes. He imagined asking her to dance. Imagined feeling her hand in his as they made their way to the dance floor. Imagined holding her close. Smelling her hair. Feeling her flesh pressed against his as they barely moved to the music, but got in tune with each other...

He swallowed hard and warned himself not to repeat past mistakes. But he was hard-pressed to obey.

He had to force himself back to the subject. "Where were we?"

Kate blinked and swallowed a mouthful of nothing. "Nathan," she choked out.

Making Chase believe he hadn't been doing all the imagining on his own.

"Right," he said. "I guess we should be taking a close look at anyone who has anything to do with the refuge, not to mention anyone who bad-mouths the land usage." His gaze strayed to the man hunkered over the bar now that Merle had deserted him. "Or anyone who has reason to dislike me personally. Buck, for one."

"I did think it was a little weird that he was working for you."

"Being lame in an area of the country where most jobs depend on a body's being fit is a serious drawback. Considering my part in what happened to Buck, I couldn't turn him down when he came to me for work this spring."

Chase glanced over at the bar again even as Buck pivoted on his stool and waved someone over. Whit Spivey had just walked through the door. A mean smile cracking his leathery face and showing off his rotting teeth, Spivey joined Buck and signaled the bartender to give them both drinks, the unexpected camaraderie giving Chase a peculiar feeling. He'd never noticed the men being particularly friendly with each other before.

What had changed?

Kate interrupted the thought, saying, "Buck does seem to have put the past behind him. And then there's Doc. Buck wouldn't kill the man who saved his life."

Only half listening, Chase frowned. "When did this happen?"

Giving him a strange look in return, she said, "The accident."

Something Chase couldn't forget. But he wasn't aware of what had gone on after he'd made it to the barns. He'd hightailed it out of there the moment he'd heard Buck blaming him. He'd been used to being a scapegoat, and his fear had been stronger than his remorse.

"What did Doc have to do with anything?" he asked, the words turning to glue in his mouth.

"He was tending to some livestock on the ranch that day. Buck might have lost his foot and more if Doc hadn't acted quickly and rode with him to the hospital. The surgeon said he saved Buck's leg."

"He's still a cripple."

"He has a limp and a scar. Lots of people deal with worse. His limp might limit his job availability, but that doesn't stop him from leading a normal life."

"Can't see much normal about it." The burger suddenly tasted like cardboard. He set the last of it down. "A grown man working a job for a kid's wages and grateful for the chance at that." Not that he wouldn't pay the man a decent wage if he could. "Plus everyone likes him and I don't figure he's hard on the eyes to females, yet he's never been married."

"What about you? You could be describing yourself."

"You're saying people like me, or that I'm not hard on the eyes?"

"I'm saying you've made choices just as Buck has. You work for no wages and you're not married, either."

"Sure about that, are you?"

Her mouth gaped open a moment, long enough for him to envision kissing it. From there his thoughts strayed to other parts of her he'd like to taste. He really couldn't keep his mind where it belonged when he was around Kate.

"*Are* you married?" she demanded.

Making him think his answer mattered to her. "Nope."

"Have you ever been?"

"Nope."

"You're not telling me you've sworn off women, are you?"

He had to grin. "Nope."

"Then what?"

The simple truth . . . "They weren't you."

Confusion warred with embarrassment and maybe anger. Suddenly Kate couldn't look at him. Chase readied himself for more accusations, but she said nothing, only concentrated on her food.

In a better mood himself, he finished his meal, then signaled Ina that he was ready to pay.

But was he ready to start something with Kate that he figured he couldn't finish? Certain he would have heard her thoughts on the subject by now if she knew the whole truth about the past, Chase had no doubt

Kate wouldn't take it kindly. And with the past still between them, they had no hope for the future.

If they had a future to look forward to, Chase reminded himself. His racing hormones and romantic notions would have to take a back seat to a more pressing dilemma.

Finding a murderer and staying alive while they did so.

Chapter Eight

Having rested for a few hours at Chase's place before
setting off on their midnight exploit, Kate felt positively energized by the time they left the cabin. Chase,
too, had slept some, though he was more grouchy than
refreshed. Giving him time to mellow out, she trailed
along behind him to the corral gate.

The first to wake, she'd caught him flat on his back
on the couch, as unmoving as a dead man. His exhaustion apparent, she'd hated to disturb him. Indeed, she hadn't for a few minutes, rather had gotten
her fill of staring at him.

With his features relaxed, thick black lashes brushing his broad cheekbones, he was almost classically
handsome. Asleep and without responsibility pressing down on him, he possessed a boyish quality she
remembered all too well. Though she stopped herself
from touching the unfamiliar scar above his right
cheekbone, she couldn't force back a fleeting memory of another night—the only other time she'd
watched him dream.

As much for her own peace of mind as for the mission, she'd awakened him.

And a cup of coffee later, he was ready to roll.

Leading one of the horses from the corral, Chase said, "Her name's Calamity."

His dark shirt was buttoned to his neck and he wore a jacket against the cool night. The red roan rolled her eyes and lipped the denim of his sleeve until he scratched her nose from its soft tip to the middle of her forehead. Then he handed the lead to Kate.

"She has a mind of her own and can get into trouble if you don't keep a firm grip on her." Turning away, he mumbled, "Like some women I know," loud enough for her to hear.

"I suspect Calamity and I will get along like old friends," Kate assured him.

To be certain, she spent a few moments bonding with the mustang, whispering in her ear and finding her sweet spots. The roan blew softly against Kate's favorite light wool jacket, its design of silhouetted horses running across a background the same blood-red as her shirt. She silently visited with Calamity until she was positive they were on the same wavelength.

And for once, she and Chase seemed to be on the same wavelength, too, Kate thought, bridling the mare.

Wondering at how easily he'd given in to her accompanying him, she wasn't about to question the opportunity. Chase might be making a valiant attempt at running the refuge single-handedly, but perhaps he was finally overwhelmed by so much pressure.

He did seem to feel the need to be in charge of everything, Kate mused as she smoothed the blanket across Calamity's withers and set the saddle in place.

"Ready?" Chase asked, riding up alongside her.

Kate fastened the cinch. "If you are."

But her thoughts continued in the same vein as they cut across the refuge toward Lockridge Acres. His need to be in control seemed to permeate every corner of his life, as illustrated by the set-to they'd had upon leaving Rowdy's.

"Why wouldn't you let me pay for supper?" she asked, remembering how irritable he'd been when she'd suggested he let her take care of the check.

"I pay my own way."

"You paid mine, too," she reminded him.

"A burger and a beer won't break me."

"Big words from a man who doesn't take a salary for his work."

"I said I didn't take a salary. I never said I was broke."

Not the first time he made her curious about the source of his folding money.

"So what did you do? Win big at poker or something?"

"Or something," he agreed.

Figuring he'd get all wound up again if she hounded him, she didn't press him and so was surprised when he continued.

"When my uncle died, he left me a stake in his ranch. I didn't figure it was fair to my cousins, so I refused to horn in on their inheritance. They figured I earned a share, and since I wouldn't take the land, they set up a bank account. Not enough to save the refuge, but enough for me to get along on."

That he confided in her pleased Kate. Made her think that, with time, he'd tell her other, more important details about the past.

After that, they rode mostly in silence. Listening to the occasional whinny of mustangs, the distant call of coyotes, the quiver of broad-leaved trees in the wind, Kate didn't mind. In tune with nature, she was for the moment content.

They approached the Lockridge place from a different direction than the one they'd taken the day before. The panorama spread before them was different, too: acre after acre of wilderness with no sign of human intervention except for the fencing.

Eventually a gate appeared, and Chase hopped down. From a saddlebag, he produced the tools to cut the chain. Rather than leaving the evidence of their break-in in plain sight, he carried the broken chain a few dozen yards away and tucked it under a clump of tall squirreltail. Even knowing they could be arrested for trespassing didn't faze Kate. Her anticipation of what they might find was growing by the minute.

Once inside, they sought out the stretch of land broken by ravines and small canyons that they'd seen through the binoculars. Another half mile or so and they halted on a small rise in the shelter of some ponderosa pine.

"Let's make sure we don't have company before riding out into the open," Chase said.

Since they'd left the refuge, an occasional cloud had scudded across the night sky, blocking the moon and throwing a deep impenetrable shadow over the land. At the moment, however, all was clear. Moonbeams limned the inert expanse before them with a silver glow.

"As long as the clouds cooperate, we'll be able to spot anything that moves," Kate said.

"The same goes for anyone else around ... so don't get sloppy."

Knowing Chase had her best interests at heart, she chose not to take offense. Normally an easygoing person, she'd been quick to anger around him—due, she was certain, to their history. She needed to get beyond that.

But how could she when other responses to him came too naturally for her comfort? Like that moment in Rowdy's when people and sounds had receded, leaving her alone with Chase and familiar feelings she hadn't wanted to consider. More and more, she was being sucked backward to a time when her heart had been whole and anything had been possible. When her mind hadn't been touched by doubt and fear.

She'd had years to harden herself to him. In a matter of days, he was breaking down her barriers.

What to do?

"Follow me," Chase said, taking Deadwood down a sloping path into the first of a series of ravines cut only by a trickle of water.

Follow him.

Once she would have followed him anywhere. She'd understood fear and his feelings of inadequacy had made him run, rather than face the horror of that accident. If he had asked, she would have run with him to the ends of the earth, naive fifteen-year-old that she'd been . . .

Deadwood's whinny drew a responding squeal from Calamity and jarred Kate out of the past.

"Whoa," Chase ordered softly.

His mount danced to one side. Hers nervously backed up, throwing her head and snorting in displeasure.

"What is it?" Kate whispered, for she saw nothing alarming.

"Got me."

They both dismounted and drew their horses into the shelter of some rocks and brush even as a cloud stole across the moon. Absolute dark prevailed, and within the womblike texture of the night, the mustangs remained disquieted. Kate felt her way between them, and with steady hands and an unspoken resolve, coaxed them into remaining silent.

Gradually the inky blackness lifted, and Kate could see that Chase was on the alert.

Then he looked her way and shook his head. "Don't see or hear anything."

Stroking Calamity's neck, Kate closed her eyes and gleaned a quick impression.

She wrinkled her nose and said, "The smell. The horses don't like the stench of this place." Uneasy, she met Chase's gaze. "Fetid...like death."

He looked disturbed and seemed to be searching inside *her*. Seconds passed without her taking a breath. Then, apparently satisfied she wasn't being unnecessarily melodramatic, he nodded and she was able to breathe normally once more.

"How do you do that?"

She shrugged. "I can't explain it. Picking up impressions is something I've always done without thinking. Delbert Lantero's the one who taught me to go deeper. To communicate with animals on a more interactive level."

He shook his head. "What I wouldn't give to have that gift."

"And there've been times in my life I would've gladly given it away."

"Why?"

"Because it made me different."

If Chase had any thoughts on the matter, he didn't offer them—maybe because he, too, had been apart from the crowd, if in a disparate way.

He sniffed the air and shook his head. "Could be a cougar, from the horses' reaction. The smell's not obvious to us, so whatever it was probably has been dead for some time. We should move on."

They remounted and picked their way deeper into the series of twisting ravines and blind canyons, tumbling with rock formations and crumbling outcrops. Vegetation flourished in the area despite the low water flow of a drier-than-usual summer. Kate realized a partially overgrown path ran mere yards from the stream bed. Vehicles had been through here, so the area must be used. But for what purpose?

Every so often, their horses renewed their protest, but neither balked. Their willingness to continue eased Kate's mind about any imminent danger. Unfortunately, however, while she tuned in to the frequent scurry of smaller wildlife around them, she had no sense of other horses nearby. And even if she and Chase missed the signs, she knew their mounts would pick out any fellow mustangs.

It wasn't until they'd gone deep into the heart of the natural maze that she caught sight of a clearing and a man-made structure. "Look."

Apparently Chase had already seen, for he was heading toward the large animal pen that stood empty. Once there, he rose in his stirrups and scanned the surrounding area.

"What the hell!" he growled, pointing.

Kate glanced behind her to a steel-barred enclosure sheltered by a small stand of birch. "A cage?"

As they moved closer to the cage, both horses began dancing, protesting, throwing up heads with eyes rolling. Before she had a chance to figure out what exactly had them so hot and bothered, Kate heard the roar of an engine from the path they'd just traveled.

"Someone's coming!"

They scurried for cover, finding a clear pocket behind an amalgamation of rocks matted with virgin's bower and surrounded by taller growth. They leapt to the ground, their footfalls deadened by short grasses. Chase slipped his rifle from his saddle, leaving the horses to her care.

As the roar of the engine drew closer, Kate touched the mustangs, cleared her mind and concentrated on relaying calm and safety to the hyper animals.

Quiet... no need for alarm... settle down... that's the way...

The words, if spoken, would be meaningless, though a gentle reassuring tone might have gotten through to them. But her physical connection and unspoken language worked faster and more thoroughly. As if hypnotized, both horses settled down and relaxed.

Kate could only wish she was equally at ease, especially when the vehicle stopped nearby and she heard doors open and several people exit.

"Here we are—the staging area," Thea Lockridge announced, a definite edge to her voice.

Thea must have brought her friends from Rowdy's for some late-night excursion. Pulse lurching, Kate grew alarmed. What in the world did the blonde expect to show anyone in the dark? Or were their intentions more sinister?

Unsure of what they'd stumbled into, Kate shivered and drew closer to Chase, thankful he was armed.

THEA WAS CERTAIN that bringing the men to her special place would close the deal. On the drive over, she'd tantalized them with possibilities. If the other amenities hadn't induced the thrill seekers to buy into her private enterprise, this should be the frosting on the cake.

Chocolate frosting, she amended, as a cloud slid in front of the moon and their world went dark.

"Hey, who turned off the lights?" Sam complained.

Thea laughed at the big man's petulant tone. "This isn't the city. No glow of skyline lights. When it gets dark out here, it's for real." Hoping to excite them, she lowered her voice and let it throb. "Danger could lurk anywhere—even behind you—and you wouldn't know it."

"We could use those fancy gadgets the army developed for 'Nam." Rather than being excited in a positive way, Larry sounded nervous. "You know, the binoculars that let you see in the dark."

"Night-vision goggles, idiot."

"I'll idiot you—"

"Now, now, boys," Thea soothed. "No fighting. Save your primal energies for more productive activities. Actually we do have several pairs of night-vision goggles and binoculars. You can't miss a thing with those babies."

Sounding relieved, Larry said, "So let's try them out."

"We'd have to return to the gun room at the compound."

"Forget it," Sam groused. "We go back to the house and I'm in bed."

The moon slid from behind the clouds and Thea went on with her sales pitch. "As you may have noticed, the area is suitably secluded—"

"Hank should be here." Larry sounded disgusted. "Too bad he let himself get distracted."

"There's no accounting for taste," a disappointed Thea said. "I would have thought a man of Hank's caliber would be a bit more discerning than to pick up a whore. However, as long as he doesn't talk in his sleep..."

Larry snorted. "Who says Hank'll be sleeping with her?"

Both men laughed and smacked each other on the back. Wincing, Thea tried to remain philosophical. Too much to expect that the creatures drawn to her concept would be as sophisticated as their polished exteriors implied. What did she care? Her interest was in the green of their money.

A nearby scuffle and thunk followed by a shushing of grass put her on the alert. "Shh." Pulse thrumming, she pricked up her ears and listened.

"Probably some animal," Sam said.

"Some *wild* animal." Larry sounded nervous again.

But Thea wasn't so certain. The hair on the back of her neck prickled in warning. She could have sworn the source was a horse. But none of the horses should be here now.

When the noise wasn't repeated, she chose not to make a big deal in front of potential buyers. No need to alert them, especially when it was probably a false alarm. Just in case, though, she would put the cell phone in the truck to good use and call her foreman. Once alerted that some horse might be loose, he'd have a select handful of men checking over the area in no time.

To that end, she suggested, "Why don't we go back to the house for a nightcap?"

The friends agreed, but as they climbed into the truck, Sam asked, "How can we be certain our privacy would be protected?"

"I run a discreet operation. And I have a business relationship with the right people. But as a further safeguard, I plan to buy adjoining property," she said, thinking of the refuge.

Thea knew she had to be careful how she handled things so as not to raise suspicions, but she was determined to get her hands on that land.

One way or another...

CHASE EXPELLED a long-held breath as Thea's four-wheel drive hightailed it out of the clearing. "That was close. I thought Calamity was going to give us away."

"My fault," Kate admitted. "I should have stayed with them. Sorry."

He hadn't been sorry she'd sought his comfort. Instinctively she'd moved close to him, had touched him without self-consciousness. And even in their tense situation, her very nearness had distracted him until Calamity had gotten restless. Kate had responded instantly, however, quieting the roan with her magic. Amazing.

She handed over Deadwood's reins and they moved back into the open. Certain she wouldn't be appreciative now that the threat of danger had passed, he fought the urge to wrap a protective arm around her.

"Why do you think Thea brought those men out here?" she asked, an edge to her voice.

"To close some real-estate deal."

"Okay, but why in this place and why at night?"

Good question. One he couldn't answer. Just as he couldn't say for sure what the enclosure and cage were doing in the middle of nowhere. He could make an intelligent guess, though, and that made his stomach churn.

"I really don't like this."

"Neither do I." Kate took a long look at the cage, then at him. Forehead furrowed, she said, "Tell me what you're thinking."

Chase inhaled deeply and went over the facts as he saw them. "The place is purposely secluded. Our horses have weird reactions to the area, due, as you said, to the smell of death. Then we find this large animal pen, not to mention a cage. And Thea talks about night-vision goggles."

"Remember the animal trophies decorating her home?" Kate waited a beat, then, "Illegal hunts?"

Their minds were in tune. Not that Chase was surprised. He'd always given Kate credit for smarts.

"We don't have proof."

"Even if we did, what could we do about it? She spoke of having a business relationship with the right people—undoubtedly Thea was indicating she has the law in her pocket."

"Pocketbook," Chase amended.

"So what do we do?"

"Put our suspicions on hold until we have time to deal with them. The mustangs are still missing," he reminded her. "And Doc Weber is still dead."

KATE HAD WALKED to Rowdy's Bar and Gruel and ridden to the refuge with Chase, so she had no choice but to let him see her home. Truth be told, she was glad for the company, even if she didn't feel much like talking. Their trek had spooked her good, and the reminder of Doc's death preyed on her mind.

By the time they arrived in Bitter Creek, she suspected dawn wasn't far from creeping over the horizon. She glanced at Chase, who seemed to be fighting to stay awake, and was concerned that he'd fall asleep at the wheel on the return drive.

That was why, when he pulled up in front of the house, she said, "You'd probably better come in and get some shut-eye before heading back."

"And shock your neighbors when they see the Bronco parked outside your door?"

"Neighbors" was a bit of an exaggeration, considering the Weber home stood at the far end of town where houses were on properties big enough to graze riding stock.

"I'll take the chance. And you won't even have to sleep on the couch." Thinking of the empty rooms in the old house, she added, "You can have your pick of beds."

She wasn't ready for his "There's only one bed I'm interested in."

Kate flushed and her insides stirred at Chase's intimate tone. Maybe he wasn't as tired as she'd assumed. Too late to rescind her invitation. And she was too emotionally worn-out to think of a clever response that would make light of the tension that lay between them—if, at times, it was hiding below the surface.

"Come in if you can behave yourself," she said bluntly.

When she left the truck, he did likewise.

Spending so much time with Chase was beginning to feel normal—even if the circumstances were anything but. Kate knew that backing up and getting out of her commitment was the only way to protect herself. But that was impossible. She'd gotten in too deep. Any peace she gained would be tempered by an overwhelming guilt. Too much remained at stake for her to think only of herself.

Doc's death.

The fate of the mustangs.

The well-being of anyone else who discovered the truth.

A mature adult, Kate decided she could deal with whatever curves the Fates threw her way in regard to Chase Brody. She would have to concentrate on her priorities.

To that end, they were barely inside the front door before she asked him, "Do you think Doc could have known what was going on at Lockridge Acres?"

She stooped to rough up a yawning Wrangler who'd been sleeping near the entrance waiting for her return.

"He didn't say a word to me."

"Me, neither."

Though Kate wondered if he'd entered any thoughts on the subject in his journal. Something to check on.

With a sharp whistle, she indicated the dog could go out, then waited for him in the doorway.

"If he suspected," she went on, "what if he faced Thea and threatened to blow the whistle on her?"

"Doc was smarter than that. Besides, he was killed on refuge property. Our villain came to him. More likely stumbled on him in the process of removing the mustangs and used the situation to keep Doc from talking."

Wrangler trotted back inside. Kate closed the door and moved toward the living room. Sliding out of her jacket, she tossed the garment on a stack of her unpacked boxes. Her mind lingered on the stampede. On the drive home, she'd gone over and over the memory she'd shared with Sage, but she hadn't come up with anything more telling.

"You're not saying Thea *couldn't* be responsible, are you?" she asked.

"Not at all. But at this point, let's not exclude anyone else. As far as I'm concerned, everyone is suspect until we get some kind of proof."

He had a point. Even if Thea were up to some illegal activity on her own property—added to her determination to buy a good portion of refuge land—that didn't make her guilty of murder.

"Still, Thea's a vile woman." Turning on a single table lamp to low, Kate dropped into the chair Doc had favored. The dog settled at her feet. "She even had to get in that shot about Merle, calling her a whore. Where does she—"

"Pure spite," Chase cut in quickly, his back to her. Though it was still dark outside, he was facing the windows as if he had a fine view of his surroundings. "I'm sure Thea is aware that Merle has no use for her and is willing to say anything to make Merle look bad."

Something about his clipped tone got to Kate. What he was saying was undoubtedly true. So why did she have the feeling he was uncomfortable with the topic? Appropriately suspicious where he was concerned, she let her mind take her somewhere she didn't want to go: Chase and Merle together.

In the same class in school, they'd hung around together as teenagers. Not that Kate had ever noticed anything romantic going on between them.

Still . . .

Chase moved away from the windows, but even then he remained in shadow. His being unreadable was somehow fitting. For Chase was as much of an enigma to her now as he had been when he'd abandoned her. She couldn't take anything about him at face value.

Half stretching out on the couch, he set his hat on top of the papers and books still covering the coffee table. "We never did finish our conversation about Nathan."

Which sounded like an excuse to get the topic off Merle. He must have had his share of women in the past eighteen years. Nothing to say Merle Zwick couldn't have been one of them.

"What didn't we cover?" she asked.

"Your opinion. What about Nathan's wanting the land returned to the Lakota?"

If Chase and Merle had had a thing together, Kate mused, the affair was obviously in the past or Merle wouldn't have flirted with Hank. Or maybe Merle had dumped Chase and he hadn't quite gotten over it. Not that she cared who Chase had slept with since her.

Not much.

Swallowing her uncalled-for resentment, Kate said, "There's a big difference between wanting something and making it happen."

"You know him as well as anyone. Better than I do. How much loyalty does he have to his people?"

"Who *are* Nathan's people?" she asked. "He was never overly fond of reservation life as a kid. He was always torn between his Native American and white roots. He went off to San Francisco to study fine arts and stayed away for years after graduating."

"But he's here now," Chase said, "living on the rez."

"Only because his mother died and left him her land. Artists can starve before they make a name for themselves. Moving back to the reservation might have been a matter of simple economics, rather than an indication he's suddenly become a militant activist. Besides which, you started the refuge, what—seven or eight years ago? Why would he have waited so long to start making trouble?"

"Opportunity. We've only been on real shaky ground financially for a little more than two years. Nathan first came to work for me late last summer— after the refuge was vulnerable. He had enough time to get to know the operation, to figure out what *could* go wrong. And he had the whole winter to think about it. Make plans."

Chase had already told her he couldn't afford to pay a staff during the winter months, so she knew that opportunities to do harm would have been nil then. And the trouble had begun in late spring. She'd already wondered if Nathan's being part of the refuge staff suited some dark purpose....

"Nathan was a pretty jealous kid," she admitted. "He didn't like his father paying so much attention to me, so he tried to get even whenever he could."

"I witnessed a few of those fights," Chase reminded her.

"He was always up-front about his anger, though."

"He was a kid then. He's older now. Maybe more clever about getting his way. Who knows what kind of prejudice he might have suffered away from the rez? He could see getting the land back for the Lakota as a personal vindication for things he himself suffered."

"I already thought of that," Kate admitted. "But—"

"Doc didn't save his life, too, did he?"

"Not to my knowledge." Unlike Buck, Nathan didn't owe Doc anything.

Too tired to think straight, Kate laid her head against the chair back and yawned. Suddenly the idea that a couple of amateurs could figure out who was trying to destroy the refuge seemed ludicrous to her.

Thea . . . Buck . . . Nathan . . .

Who next?

If she and Chase hashed over every possible grievance long enough, she was certain they could turn everyone else connected with the place into a viable suspect.

Annie . . . Whit . . . even Merle.

"My brain is mush. I'm waving the white flag," she groaned, allowing her tired eyes to drift closed. "I surrender."

"You'd better get to bed, then."

"What about you?"

That Chase didn't immediately answer got her attention. Whipping open her eyes, Kate realized he was towering over her. She stared up into his face, caught by a fleeting and familiar vulnerability. Suddenly aware of her heartbeat, Kate knew she should do something, say *anything* to break the tenuous connection.

No words came.

Then Chase was reaching for her. His fingers grasped her wrist and pulled her arm toward him. With sensation radiating from where his hand dominated hers, she allowed the rest of her to follow, stopping mere centimeters from their bodies colliding.

When he murmured, "I told you what interested me," the power of his meaning shuddered through her.

Kate stood transfixed, afraid to blink. Moving slowly enough that she had time to escape if she so chose, Chase slid his hand up from her wrist to her elbow, then her shoulder. He was barely touching her, yet she was feeling thoroughly seduced. Her pulse thrummed and every nerve in her body burned as if he'd set it afire.

His breath caressing her face, he ordered softly, "Kiss me, Kate."

Strangely mesmerized, she obeyed. Rising to her toes, she brushed her mouth across his. A light meeting of lips, no more.

His intake of breath was gratifying. His return kiss a sensual demand.

Too languid to fight herself, as well as Chase, Kate gave over, moving both hands up his chest and around his neck. She lost herself in the moment—became weak-kneed and light-headed, almost as if she was a little drunk. When his tongue slid into her mouth, she nuzzled it with her own.

Groaning, he crushed her to him. His hands cupped her backside. And when he tilted her into him, she knew the potency of his hunger. Instant desire washed over her—a sinking, drowning, glorious sensation.

Kate's right brain imagined Chase undressing her and making love to her where they stood. But her left brain freed her mouth of his.

Though Chase still had the power to make her want him, her own words echoed back to her: *There's a difference between wanting something and making it happen.*

Kate knew she should be routing Chase, sending him on his way. Instead, she was staring into the face she had once loved too well, more than anything wishing she could get inside his head.

How long? she wondered.

If she were to weaken completely, how long would Chase stay interested in her this time? If the refuge went the way of most good intentions, would he go with it? She certainly could imagine him riding into the sunset without ever saying a word to her.

That knowledge made her say, "You'd better go or you'll never get any sleep."

His gaze was steady. "Maybe I don't care."

"Maybe I do."

He realized she was serious. She could see it in the subtle shift of his expression. Still, he didn't let go of her immediately. He appeared torn—and for a moment, she thought he might try to convince her otherwise.

But in the end, his expression blanked and he stepped back.

And Kate endured his loss all over again.

Chapter Nine

Falling asleep well after dawn, Kate got a late start for her first appointment. She was eating breakfast on the run—Wrangler shadowing her, hoping for a tidbit—when the ringing phone stopped her from opening the front door.

She spun around, practically tripping over the dog. Annoyed, she cried, "Not under my feet!"

Wrangler hung his head and let his tail droop. Immediately contrite—her lack of sleep wasn't *his* fault—Kate offered the dog her last bite of English muffin as the phone rang a second time. Wondering if Chase might be calling, she made it to the end table and picked up the receiver before it could sound again.

"Kate Farrell."

"You're out of breath."

"Hi, Neil." Telling herself she was not disappointed at hearing her brother's voice, she explained, "I was heading out the door."

"Then I'm glad I caught you. This'll only take a minute. I heard from Keelin this morning."

Keelin McKenna. No, she amended, Keelin Leighton now. So much had happened in two days that she'd totally forgotten about the imminent arrival of her Irish cousin.

"Did Keelin tell you when she and her new husband might get into town?"

"Late this afternoon. Mom's so nervous she's already starting dinner."

"Dinner?" Kate pulled a face. She knew what that meant. "What time?"

"Seven. And she said not to be late. She won't have any excuses."

Not even her trying to find a murderer? Not that Kate would tell her family anything that would put them in a panic.

"How's Dad taking it?"

"In silence. Mom's not speaking to *him*, either."

Great. An uncomfortable meal to look forward to— *if* her father was even present. Just a little storm cloud to add more stress to her day.

At least her work went smoothly. She gave Lou Sussman's new bull a clean bill of health. Julia Blake's horse had recuperated fully from the colic. And other than having to worm them again, she found that Mark Randall's pet burros were thriving nicely on an altered diet.

Kate kept herself so busy all morning she didn't have time to think about the refuge—well, Chase— until she was consuming a late lunch she'd bought on the drive out. The ham sandwich was a little dry because the kid who'd made it had forgotten the mayo, but she was hungry enough to devour every bite and wash it down with a can of soda.

No use denying that she was weakening toward Chase. Even trying to charge up her old anger had become a futile effort. She would never forget how he'd broken her heart, but she was finally allowing herself some perspective on the situation. They'd been so young that sooner or later something had been bound to tear them apart. Her going off to college, for example. Then she would have been the one to leave Chase behind.

Of course she wouldn't have done so as callously as he had, Kate assured herself. He would have known where she was. He would have been able to call or write. They would have seen each other during her many school vacations. But in all honesty Kate couldn't say their relationship would have remained constant.

And she couldn't forget that she had fallen in love with and married another man years ago. She certainly hadn't been thinking about Chase Brody then.

But she was thinking about him now. Constantly. Why?

Pulling up to the refuge office, she chose to leave the question unanswered for the moment. Buck was just taking out an afternoon tour, while other tourists were heading for their cars. Chase's Bronco was nowhere in sight.

Kate stuffed her sandwich wrapper and empty can into a paper sack, which she took with her upon leaving the pickup. At the garbage container, she sensed a furtive movement—Annie slipping from her office onto the front porch. Without so much as a greeting, the volunteer stared at her through the screened wall. Silence thick with animosity pebbled the skin along Kate's arms.

Unable to tolerate the uncomfortable quiet, she called out, "Hey, Annie," in a normal friendly tone. She moved toward the steps, wondering what in the world had gotten the volunteer's back up. "Where did Chase get himself off to?"

"I thought you were the expert on that. You were with him all night."

Kate winced at the other woman's obvious assumption. Expression sullen, Annie opened the screen door and stood square in the opening, arms crossed over her chest as if she meant to prevent Kate from entering the building. Though she'd have liked to put the jealous woman's mind at ease, she couldn't.

All she said was, "That doesn't mean I know where he is now."

Annie's blue eyes were frosty. "He and Merle are checking over the perimeter fences."

"More trouble?"

"That's what they're looking for."

Kate took an easier breath. "Let's hope to God they don't find it."

Annie appeared to be working herself up for something Kate knew she wasn't going to like, when a shout from some distance claimed her attention.

"Hey, missy! Kate Farrell!"

Turning, she discovered Whit Spivey at the top of the incline, waving her over toward the trail-ride center. Signaling him she'd heard and would be there directly, she murmured, "I wonder what he wants."

"Money," Annie said flatly. "His only motivation."

"Money from me?"

"From anyone who'll give it to him . . . or whoever he can take it from." Seeming about to say more, Annie shook her head. "Never mind. You'd better get over there. If you ignore him, he'll pitch a fit."

Though she would have liked further explanation of the vague accusation, Kate sensed any questions would be met with more hostility.

"If Chase gets back while I'm talking to Spivey, let him know I'm here."

"I'll be sure to do that."

Kate didn't miss her bitter tone.

She felt Annie's eyes boring into her back all the way to the pickup. Glad to have something to distract her from worrying about the other woman, she sped uphill to where the trail boss waited for her, hands balled into fists on his hips,

"Took you long enough," Spivey groused as she alighted. "I got a horse needs vetting."

Though Kate was hardly acquainted with the man—Spivey had only settled in Bitter Creek a few years ago, but well before she'd moved back to town—she instinctively disliked him. Not that she would use that as an excuse to turn her back on an animal who needed her.

"What happened?"

"I hired an irresponsible kid to help me take good care of my animals is what."

Spivey stalked toward a big bay tied up away from the rest of the string. While the others were saddled, the bay was not. Kate immediately identified the problem. A gash across the gelding's flank was oozing puss.

"Oh, sweetheart," she murmured, moving toward the horse's head so he could see her and therefore be less apprehensive. "How did you hurt yourself?"

"He musta rolled on something sharp."

Frowning, Kate considered the possibility, but the wound seemed awfully large to have been inflicted that way. The metal tag on his halter identified the young gelding as Hercules. Suddenly the horse jerked away, and she realized Spivey had stepped into his line of sight. Eyes rolling, the animal pulled at his tether.

"Shh," Kate whispered, touching his velvet nose. Hercules didn't like Spivey, either. And she couldn't miss the sudden restlessness of the other horses in the string. "Settle down, Hercules, thatta boy."

She ran a gentle hand across his cheek and along his neck. While his flesh quivered, the gelding stood quiet for her. And kept an eye on the man.

Spivey spat out a wad of chewing tobacco. "Damn that Teddy for going off and not saying a thing!"

"Teddy Wyatt?"

"That's the one."

Kate frowned. Teddy was both horse crazy and one of the most responsible kids she knew. She was certain he wouldn't go off and leave a hurt animal of any sort. But saying so would only get Spivey more riled.

"I'll clean this up and start Hercules on antibiotics."

"How soon will he be able to work? I can't afford horses who don't earn their keep."

In a manner of speaking, Kate thought, Annie had been correct about what the man wanted from her. The trail boss was more concerned about making money than about the gelding's welfare.

Though she bit her tongue to keep her opinion to herself, Kate knew her voice held an edge. "You won't be able to saddle him for a few days certainly. The leather rubbing against the wound would make things worse."

"He'd better be ready for the weekend," Spivey muttered, gray eyes cold, "or else!"

Or else what?

The trail boss stalked off toward his lean-to, narrow shoulders set like steel.

"Don't you worry, sweetheart," Kate soothed, moving closer to comfort the horse and check the wound more thoroughly. "I'll tell Chase and he won't let Spivey work you until you're ready."

The flesh near the wound flinched under her fingertips and a fuzzy image formed in her mind.

A foul-tempered Whit Spivey swinging out a hand holding a thick leather strap . . .

The image distorted as a squeal of pain echoed through Kate's head.

Realizing Spivey had been the one to inflict the wound, she swore under her breath and whipped around to confront him. The moron had already disappeared into his tack house.

"I'll be right back with my bag, Hercules." Giving the gelding a piece of carrot to munch on, she assured him, "I'll make it better, I promise."

And she wasn't only talking about healing the wound itself.

"ALL I CAN DO IS TALK to him," Chase said after Kate had explained the situation. The thought of Spivey mistreating one of his horses made him sick, but other than using violence on the bastard to teach him a lesson, he didn't know what he could do. "I'll strongly suggest he treat the horses with respect or I'll—"

"What do you mean, suggest? He works for you!"

"Actually he doesn't. He's an independent contractor and owns the trail horses."

Chase could tell Kate was frustrated enough to scream. His mouth drew into a thin line. He wasn't any happier.

She paced the small office, the sheen of collecting tears lending a luminous quality to her green eyes. "Someone should take those animals away from Spivey!"

Chase knew Kate would never let her tears fall, at least not in front of him. He wanted to take her in his arms and comfort her, tell her it was all right to cry if she wanted, but he was certain she would balk at his touching her. Besides, Annie could be back at any moment, and he had a feeling showing affection to another woman in front of her would not be a good idea.

Opening his fists, he shoved his hands into his pockets and propped a hip against the edge of the desk. "You know damn well that taking legal action against him wouldn't be easy, Kate."

As difficult as it was for the law to stop men from abusing their wives and kids, he thought, remembering his own situation, it was nearly impossible to stop the abuse of animals, especially if the owner's actions weren't openly flagrant. Unfortunately Spivey was clever. He'd stick to his story about Hercules hurting himself in the pasture. And considering how Kate had gleaned her knowledge of the truth, who would believe her?

"We have to do *something!*"

"Like I said, I'll talk to him. That'll have to do for now. We have too much to deal with as it is. We can't fix everything wrong with the world at the same time."

"I suppose you're right."

"And if I learn Spivey mistreats one of those horses again, I'll take care of him myself," he promised.

"Then *you* would be the one in trouble with the law." Kate shook her head. "Why would a man who so obviously disrespects horses choose to work with them—and at a refuge meant to protect those very creatures?"

"Why do batterers marry and have children? To keep control over their victims."

Kate's mouth gaped. Then she blinked and took a deep breath, her expression subtly changing. "Chase, what about Spivey? What if he's the one who's—"

Noting a movement on the porch from the corner of his eye, he stopped her cold. "We can finish this up later." Since he didn't know who he could trust, Chase wasn't taking any chances. Casually he glanced over Kate's shoulder. "Annie, there you are."

"Were you looking for me?" she asked, entering the office and ignoring Kate.

He didn't miss the hopeful note in her voice. "Actually I was wondering how long ago Nathan left to get those supplies he wanted."

The corners of her mouth turning down, she said, "One, one-thirty. Something like that. He was planning on having lunch first."

Chase checked the wall clock. "I guess he'll be a while, then. And I'd better get on that grant application I've been avoiding."

"If Nathan calls in, should I give him a message?" Annie asked.

"No, it can wait. But thanks." To Kate he said, "I'm on my way, then. Want to walk me out?"

"Sure."

Aware of Annie's sullen gaze following them, Chase crossed the porch and left the building. The volunteer had been moody lately, and he was beginning to suspect she was taking his bond with Kate as a personal affront, though he'd never indicated anything but friendly interest toward her. The notion worried him.

"So what's this about Nathan?" Kate asked. "You're keeping tabs on him?"

"I wanted to make sure he was busy elsewhere so I could check out the renovation site. Nathan set up temporary living quarters in one of the log cabins, supposedly because he didn't want to commute to the rez."

"I didn't realize he was staying on the property. That would be convenient . . ."

"And that's why I figured on seeing if I could find anything that links him to the havoc around here."

"What do you expect to find?"

"I'll know when I see it. *If* I see it." Nathan had the benefit of his doubt.

"I've been thinking there might be something *I* didn't see," Kate mused as they arrived at his truck. She clarified, "About the stampede. They say the third time's the charm. I should locate Sage and find out if that's true in this case."

"Not without me, you don't." A surge of protective emotion coursed through Chase. Her hardheadedness had gotten her into trouble once. Next time the villain might shoot to kill. "No more solo middle-of-the-night adventures."

Her innocuous expression made him nervous. He'd expected her to react to his order with her usual affront. Even a little frown of irritation would have made him feel better.

"Tonight I have a family obligation," she informed him. "One of my McKenna cousins from Ireland is visiting. Actually Keelin met a man in Chicago whom she married this past weekend. Mom has been working on a celebratory dinner all day."

Though somewhat reassured, Chase realized he was also disappointed. "Then I won't be seeing you."

"I guess not."

Try as he might, he couldn't tell if the fact mattered to her or not. Though he'd meant to keep his distance, he'd failed. Even now he was hard-pressed not to reach out and touch the strand of bright red hair that had escaped her ponytail. He had the urge to touch her in any way he could. Kate wasn't the kind of woman a man could be neutral about.

"We have to talk," he said. And not only about the refuge. Certain she was at least softening toward him, he repressed the whisper of guilt reminding him that she might not be so amenable if she knew everything. "I'll call."

"I don't know what time I'll be home."

"Then I'll keep calling until I get you."

Not waiting for another objection, Chase jumped into the truck and sped off. If only he *could* get her. Not to mention the person responsible for Doc's death before someone else got hurt.

FEELING DUSTY and dry-mouthed, Kate washed her face and hands, shoved her wild hair under her hat and fetched herself a can of soda, which she could drink while on her way to the back reaches of the refuge. She figured everyone was occupied, so no one would pay her any mind.

Besides, even the most suspicious wouldn't expect her to go looking for Sage's band in broad daylight.

When Chase had demanded she not seek out the wild horses without him, she hadn't actually lied. Rather, she'd avoided the truth of her intentions by telling him she couldn't go that night, anyway, because of her family obligation. She'd been thinking of telling him exactly what she meant to do when he'd sprung the Nathan thing on her. With Nathan around most of the time, this might be Chase's only chance to check things out to his satisfaction.

About to climb behind the wheel, Kate noticed the dust cloud rapidly approaching and recognized the low-riding vehicle wreathed in fine red particles. *Great!* Nathan Lantero had returned earlier than anticipated. Chase hadn't even been gone ten minutes.

The can of soda clutched in one hand, she used the other to flag down Nathan before he could whiz by. To help Chase finish what he started, she would delay Nathan from returning to the renovation site for as long as possible. But how? Her mind humming as the pickup screeched to a stop, the material in the bed shifting wildly, she thought to kill two birds with one stone.

"Kate," Nathan called through the open window. "How's it going?"

She pulled a face. "Not so good."

When he quickly alighted, she noticed that while his long hair hung loose as usual, a thin braid woven with blue-and-white tile beads and decorated with a hawk's feather brushed his right cheek. And he was wearing a white raw cotton pullover shirt with billowy sleeves and a quill-and-bead necklace.

She'd never seen Nathan look quite so... Indian.

"Something happen I should know about?" he asked. "You have another vision?"

His asking didn't sit any more comfortably with her than did his appearance.

"This isn't about the refuge," Kate said evasively. "I'm concerned about one of Whit Spivey's horses. All of them actually," she amended truthfully.

"Spivey!" Nathan spit out the name as if trying to rid himself of a foul taste. "What's he done now?"

"He asked me to tend to a hurt trail horse. He tried telling me the wound was accidental—his rolling on something that cut him."

"But you don't believe it."

She shook her head. "Spivey used a leather strap on the poor animal."

"How do you...?" Nathan's question faded off as he apparently realized that she'd gotten the visual impression from Hercules. His expression narrowed in disgust. "Doesn't surprise me none."

"I was wondering...have you noticed anything else wrong with the other trail horses?"

"One came up lame a few weeks ago. Bruised bone, Spivey said. And before that, another had a problem with an eye."

More information than she'd actually expected to get from him. "What kind of problem?"

"The eye was swollen and half-closed, like someone had punched it good."

Visualizing the mean-spirited man punching out one of his horses, Kate felt her stomach roil. "Something needs to be done to put Whit Spivey out of the trail-ride business for good, but that would be impossible without proof. Do you think anyone might have seen him mistreat any of his animals?"

"Never heard. Teddy's the one to talk to, though if he saw something out of line, I'd bet the kid would've told Chase right away."

Her heart sank to her toes. "That's what I was thinking."

"You can't fix everything that's broke, Kate."

An echo of Chase's words. "No kidding."

Just as she was wondering how to stall him a while longer, the solution came from Nathan himself.

"So you saw Spivey hitting his horse."

Instinctively she knew he was really interested in what she might have seen through Sage. He'd warned her against seeking out the mare again. And now he wanted confirmation one way or another.

What if he *did* know?

With temporary quarters on the refuge, Nathan could have spotted and followed her. He could have fired off those shots as a warning.

What he *couldn't* know was whether or not she'd picked up on anything incriminating.

And she wasn't about to satisfy his curiosity.

"I had a quick flash of Spivey wielding the strap," Kate said, and rather than lie outright, she circumvented the certainty of a more direct question. "I don't go around having visions on a daily basis, you realize."

Though Nathan didn't challenge the statement, he looked down his straight blade of a nose at her. Kate grew uncomfortable under his stare, fearing he was trying to connect with her so he could read her mind for himself. Determined to keep him off a subject she didn't intend to discuss, she figured out a way to turn the tables on him.

"Say...Annie told me something that surprised me."

"What's that?"

"She said the Lakota had been trying to make a deal with the governor to buy this land when Chase came up with his proposal for the refuge."

"True enough. And we should have gotten it."

Kate didn't miss the *we*. Glancing at the decorated braid, she asked, "When did you develop such a commitment to the same people you once fled from?"

Again Nathan stared, and she had to stop herself from flinching under his black gaze. Though he'd threatened her many times as a kid, she'd never feared him.

Now she did.

"When I learned what was important in the world," he finally said. He turned his back on her and climbed into his vehicle. "I gotta get to work."

"Sorry. I guess I've been holding you up."

Kate only hoped long enough for Chase to complete his search.

NOT HAVING BEEN to the renovation site for weeks, since all his spare time had been consumed with fixing engines, repairing fences and hunting down missing horses—not to mention pursuing the elusive villain—Chase took a few minutes to inspect Nathan's work before beginning his search.

At first glance, the outside of the old log buildings looked to be originals. The pine logs themselves were authentic if refinished, but modern mortar blocked the chinks, cedar shingles replaced sod roofs, and the windows were of glass, instead of mica or waxed paper.

But the small details Nathan had added on his own, particularly those on the main house, made the place come alive: hand-carved porch posts, handcrafted mica and metal lamps hanging above front doors, original design worked into the stone chimneys.

Hard to believe that a man doing such exceptional and creative work could also have a bent for destruction.

Knowing he had no alternative but to break some personal rules to get to the truth—a man's right to his privacy being at the top of his list—Chase headed for Nathan's personal quarters.

Nathan had chosen to occupy the smallest of the half-dozen log buildings and had built a corral for his horse nearby. Chase clucked softly at the medicine hat—a type of paint with a white face, dark ears and dark patch on its chest favored by Indians in the nineteenth century. The gelding snorted at him and went back to his grazing.

Chase hadn't been inside the cabin since Nathan had taken temporary possession of the single-room structure. As he'd expected, the door was unlocked. Surprisingly the room was even more sparsely outfitted than he'd imagined. Simple bedding lay on the newly installed wood floor. The furniture consisted of a large antique trunk and a bookshelf, as well as a table, bulletin board and chair that provided a workstation. All were lined up along the same wall.

On closer inspection, the books proved to be of a single topic—Native Americans, emphasis on Sioux history and culture, two recounting Wounded Knee. Sketches pinned to the board were of Indian men and women in traditional dress. A work-in-progress on the table was that of a heavily armed warrior. Staring at the sketches, then back at the book titles, he felt his mouth go dry.

Nathan's sole interest didn't bode well. As much as he wanted to, Chase didn't think he'd be able to eliminate the other man as a suspect.

His gaze strayed to the trunk. Hesitating only a moment, he knelt in front of it, releasing the old-fashioned catches and lifting the heavy lid. Inside, several artifacts lay on quilted padding.

A stuffed kingfisher decorated with beads and feathers.

An ash bow strung with buffalo sinews in a buckskin case with an attached quiver of arrows.

A sandstone-headed club decorated with horsehair.

A quilled breastplate.

A rawhide shield stretched over a frame, adorned with the carcass of a small bird of prey, hawk feathers and horsetail.

A bonnet of bearskin and eagle feathers.

The significance of the artifacts hit Chase like a Mack truck.

All articles of war.

Chase sat back on his heels and took a deep breath. No expert, he knew a little of Native American lore. As a magic charm, the kingfisher symbolized quickness and helped the warrior to dodge arrows. The war bonnet gave him super human powers needed to survive—the bear being a personal guardian, the eagle a predator.

He set the trunk lid in place and stood, again staring at the sketches pinned to the board as if he could fathom whether or not Nathan Lantero was the predator determined to destroy the refuge.

Chase eventually became aware of a presence behind him.

Because he suspected Nathan could be armed, he turned slowly. No jerky movements that could be misinterpreted. The other man blocked the doorway, his arms folded across his chest. As far as Chase could tell, he wasn't carrying a weapon. The bright light behind Nathan threw his face into shadow—Chase couldn't even guess what he might be thinking.

Not having any way to know how much the other man had observed, he bluffed, "I finally made the time to check on your progress."

"Find what you wanted?" Nathan asked dryly.

"Reassurance that things are going smoothly? You bet. Everything looks good."

"In here, too?"

Chase ignored the verbal dare. "Your work is more than satisfactory, but I think you know that."

"I know lots of things," Nathan agreed, finally stepping out of the doorway. "If you have questions...ask."

Another challenge, this one more direct. "So, did you get all the supplies you needed?"

Nathan's expression was devoid of emotion, but he couldn't hide the flicker of surprise that lit his dark gaze.

"I have everything I need," he agreed. "For now."

Chase nodded. "I was admiring your handiwork— the sketches, as well as what you're doing for the refuge. I didn't realize you'd gone back to your art."

"A new project," Nathan said. "I got inspired."

"By anything in particular?"

"Now, if I said, 'by the possibility of making money,' you'd be disappointed, wouldn't you?"

Not really an answer. And Chase knew he wasn't going to get one that was any more direct.

EXPERIENCE HAD TAUGHT Kate that tracking down Sage's band wouldn't be too difficult. The tough part had come in calculating how to glean any information she might have missed. The last time, the images had flown by too quickly. Deciding that if she wanted to see more—the villain, hopefully—she needed to keep the mare calm. She'd asked herself what Doc would do and immediately thought of the treat that had been his favorite to dispense.

Sweetened grain mash. Evidence had shown he'd brought along a bucket of the stuff the night he'd died.

Balanced on a boulder next to the creek, she dangled her pail before her. "You know what this is, don't you?" she cooed.

Having answered her whistle, Sage and the other girls had come closer, yet still remained at some distance. Considering what had happened last time, she didn't blame them. But upon seeing the bucket, Sage lifted her nose and sniffed, then meandered toward her, looking this way and that, much as a cat would do to pretend disinterest.

One of the other mares was not so reluctant, and within seconds, Kate was surrounded, her filled palm snuffled by a velvety nose. She made certain the girls shared whether or not they wanted to.

"C'mon, Sage, stop being a party pooper."

The mare finally made up her mind and shouldered her way past the others. Eyeing Kate with only a touch of suspicion, she dipped her head and lipped the grain mash.

"Thatta girl. I knew you'd like it."

Kate scooped a larger handful and carefully set down the bucket. Snorting, Sage went for seconds, while Kate smoothed the silky neck with her free hand. Then, conjuring up an image she'd seen a million times—Doc with bucket in one hand, a horse eating from the other—she closed her eyes and concentrated, zeroing in on Doc's smiling face, silently telegraphing the image to the mare.

They connected...

...and suddenly Doc appeared older... the indigo sky behind him streaked with sheet lightning... her being bumped by other horses...

Excitement rushed through Kate as she realized this was an earlier memory, one preceding the stampede. Calming herself, she tuned back in.

...a howl... followed by a different sound... Doc turning away...

Pulse thrumming, Kate recognized the chugging noise. The engine of a truck. Not a personal vehicle but a commercial one.

...high beams... Doc limping away from the corral... panicked whinnying...

The warning set Kate's neck hair to attention.

...a hazy form silhouetted between the truck's high beams and the hot sheet lightning... a brighter, more blinding ray flicking on...

Startled out of Sage's memory, Kate felt as if her heart were pounding right out of her chest. She'd seen someone driving a truck, rather than riding a horse. Dear Lord, why hadn't she and Chase thought of this before? All this time they'd been trying to pin the nefarious doings on a single person.

Now she knew for certain that two of them were involved!

Chapter Ten

Kate burned with the need to talk to Chase all through the family gathering. Though she'd tried calling him several times to share her new insight before sitting down at the dinner table, he'd remained elusive. She only prayed that Nathan hadn't walked in on Chase going through his things....

So distracted, Kate only gradually became aware that—between bites of roast beef, seasoned potatoes, a snap-bean casserole, fresh biscuits and other treats—her cousin Keelin was doing a fine job of engaging her father in conversation whether he'd meant to speak to her or not.

"Despite the many miles between us, Uncle Charlie, our families have much in common," Keelin was saying, a sweet smile lending a radiant beauty to her somewhat ordinary features and lighting her soft gray eyes.

"How so?"

"My siblings and I grew up on a dairy farm, while you raised your children on a cattle ranch. There are three of us, as well."

''I expect that makes us similar to a good percentage of the families in the civilized world,'' Charlie said gruffly.

Kate exchanged a look with Neil, who succeeded in keeping a straight face—until he glanced at their Irish cousin. Then he could do so no longer. Keelin's dark auburn hair rained down along the shoulders of a loose dress the yellow of sagebrush buttercups found in the wooded marshy areas of the Black Hills. Kate thought she'd bring a bright spot to the darkest day.

'' 'Tis true,'' Keelin went on. ''But is it not a grand feeling to know you have such connections?''

''My connections are all right here,'' Charlie argued. ''Except for my son Quin, who keeps running around getting himself into hot water, of course. Next thing I know, you'll be comparing me to James McKenna!''

''Charlie, hush!''

''Don't hush me at my own table, Rose—''

''Da *can* be a difficult one,'' Keelin said, stopping the argument cold. ''When he takes a stand, he will dig in. But he is a good man with human failings like the rest of us.''

Kate was aware of Keelin glancing at Tyler, giving him a look that was half reproachful, half teasing, as if she'd had personal experience with *his* shortcomings, too. And yet...she'd married him, anyway. Love conquering all?

Unbidden, Chase came to mind.

''And though Da does not often admit when he is wrong,'' Keelin was saying, her lilt mesmerizing, ''his heart has never been the same since his family became...disconnected.''

''By me, you mean,'' Charlie groused.

"By his own weaknesses. Growing up in a country divided by religious and political differences can twist a man's thinking. Perhaps you need to experience such confusion firsthand before you can truly understand."

"The United States has its problems—"

"But it's not at war with itself, Dad," Neil pointed out.

"Not in the same manner," Tyler agreed. "Especially not out here."

Keelin put a hand on Tyler's arm. "I cannot speak for you, Uncle Charlie. I can only say that *I* would give any decent person who made a terrible error in judgment a second chance." Before he could find a way to object, she turned to her aunt. "Such a lovely dinner, Aunt Rose. I only hope you didn't spend your entire day in the kitchen because of our arrival."

"Oh, no, of course not. This is just a run-of-the-mill Farrell family dinner."

Hand over her mouth to hold in her snicker, Kate exchanged another significant look with her brother, who was hiding his smile behind a napkin. That their mother glowed from the inside out thrilled Kate. Keelin was good medicine for Mom. And maybe for Dad, as well.

Her Irish cousin seemed to have a keen insight on people, and her belief in second chances nagged at Kate through the rest of the meal.

ALL COMPLAINING they were stuffed, the men retired to Dad's study, while Mom insisted on loading the dishwasher herself.

Wanting a few minutes alone with Keelin, Kate had volunteered to give her cousin a tour of the grounds.

As they strolled through the barn, they fed carrot sticks to the riding horses, who'd already been brought in against possible bad weather.

"Why are you really here, Keelin?"

"This is my marriage trip."

"You didn't even know Tyler when you came to the States," Kate reminded her, leading the way outside to the accompaniment of snorted protests. "You went to see Skelly and Aileen and Uncle Raymond in Chicago. Now you're here."

"I cannot be fooling you, I see. I want Da, Aunt Rose and Uncle Raymond to be reunited."

Kate grinned. "Good. I was trying to figure out how to get Mom to go back to Ireland for a visit myself."

"So you think she would be amenable?"

"I'm certain she would. Dad's the problem." Kate sighed. "Mom's always had her moods over what happened with her brothers. I think it made her sick inside. And it's stopped her and Dad from being truly happy together. No matter how much they love each other, there's this invisible wall at times... Lately, I think Mom has been worried that if she isn't reunited with James and Raymond soon, it'll be too late."

"My very thought," Keelin admitted. "Da recently had a heart attack."

"Oh, Keelin..."

"He'll be doing fine, God willing. But when he was at his most desperate, he called out for Raymond and Rose. Of course, now that he's recovered, he'll not be admitting to his heart's desire. I know having all his family around him would give Da the resolve to live forever. That's why I'm wanting a family reunion—all the McKennas and their loved ones together."

A fleeting image of her holding Chase's hand in the midst of her extended family put a lump in Kate's throat. "When?"

"In time to celebrate our parents' sixtieth birthday."

"Perfect. Exactly what Mom needs." Kate frowned, thinking she should warn her cousin. "If Dad pressures her, I'm not sure she'll agree. Then again...you practically had him eating out of your hand."

Keelin's eyes widened. "And I thought I had irritated him beyond reason."

"Trust me, you did good."

Kate stopped before a fenced pasture where several mares grazed with their foals. The sun was in the process of setting, and the sky had darkened to a purple streaked with pink and orange. In the far, far distance, faint streaks of lightning stabbed through thick clouds to touch the earth. Her familiar whistle brought the mothers nearer, the long-legged babies shadowing them. Then she clucked softly until a blue roan boldly stuck her nose through the split rails.

Watching Kate closely, Keelin said, "You remind me of my brother Curran. He has a gift with the horses. He trains Thoroughbreds for a well-known Irish stable."

The wind soughed around them, plucking and pushing at her. Kate hesitated only a moment. "Speaking of gifts, how well did you know our grandmother?" She gave the mare a carrot stick.

"Better than anyone."

"Could Moira really communicate with animals?"

"Among other talents."

As Kate stroked the mare, she automatically checked her out, turning inward until a feeling of wellness and contentment filled her. She smiled and patted the roan.

"You have the touch, as well, don't you?" Keelin asked, sounding a bit awed.

Surprised that her cousin had known what she was up to, Kate said, "That I do." She distributed carrot sticks among the other mares, who'd responded to her whistle.

Keelin laughed happily. "Oh, my, and I thought I was the only one."

"You're able to connect with animals, too?"

"I inherited a different ability from our grandmother." Keelin sobered. "I sometimes dream through another's eyes—dreaming what they are seeing at that very moment. I don't mind when the visions are pleasant, but that has not always been the case. I've seen terrible things, Kate—people in desperate trouble."

Lightning flickered in the distance as if for emphasis, sending a chill through Kate and reminding her of her current situation. "I can empathize. The responsibility gets to you, right?"

Keelin nodded. "The first time it happened, I declared that I wanted nothing to do with such a burden. Gran told me that I was chosen because I was strong enough to meet the challenge. No matter. For most of my life, I thought this gift a curse. And yet, if I'd not had it... Tyler's daughter, Cheryl, had been kidnapped and somehow, across an ocean and half a continent, I saw through her eyes in my dreams."

"That's how you met Tyler?"

"Aye. Thank heaven I helped rescue his child, but only after pushing my gift beyond the boundaries I'd known before."

Suddenly Kate felt less alone with her own burden. "I'm so glad things turned out positively." Both for Cheryl and for Keelin.

The air had become chilly and damp, and the sky had grown dark. Though often the threatening weather zigzagged around them, there was no use taking chances and getting caught in a downpour.

"Maybe we should get back before the skies open."

"I don't melt when I get wet," Keelin said with a laugh. "Eire has more than its share of rain."

"Not like we have, it doesn't. Have you ever seen hail the size of softballs?"

Keelin went wide-eyed. "Perhaps we should hurry."

Both laughing, they set off arm in arm, Kate saying, "You really love Tyler, don't you?"

"More than life itself."

Feeling closer to Keelin than a cousin, almost as if she'd found the sister she'd always longed for, she asked, "What if the man you loved did something really awful? Could you forgive him and love him, anyway?"

A haunted expression flashed through Keelin's eyes. "I would consider all the circumstances. And I would look to see what kind of person he really was. I would ask myself which was the more important—a single deed or the whole of the man. And most of all, Kate, I would ask myself whether or not I felt true love for him."

Keelin sensed what she herself hadn't wanted to concede, Kate realized. She'd admitted to being in lust with the man, but she hadn't asked herself how she felt about Chase deep in her heart, because she'd been afraid of the answer. Now she was afraid the answer was becoming all too obvious.

"None of us is perfect or we would all be part of the heavenly choir," Keelin said. "I believe we were put on earth to make ourselves the best human beings possible. Unfortunately some of us have to work harder than others to become all we can."

And Chase's father had given him a hellish start, Kate knew. So many victims succumbed to a life of misery and never found their way out. Chase had fought back. Perhaps he hadn't always done the correct thing, but he had kept fighting and he had changed. Any woman should be proud to love the man he had become.

"Kate, may I ask you something personal?"

Thinking Keelin's curiosity was about her relationship with Chase, she said, "Of course."

"Earlier this evening I sensed you were troubled by something. I was wondering about the source. Perhaps I can help."

Not wanting to alert the rest of her family, Kate stopped in the shelter of an outbuilding before they reached the house. She found herself telling Keelin about the problems plaguing the refuge and gave her a shorthand version of her stormy relationship with Chase Brody.

She told her about Doc and how, through Sage, she'd come to realize his death hadn't been an accident.

And about her determination to bring the villain to justice.

"I can't let this rest, Keelin, no matter how dangerous it might become. I have to keep on for Doc's sake."

"And for Chase."

"And for Chase," Kate echoed softly, realizing it was true.

Even knowing that if the refuge did fail, he might turn around and walk straight out of her life again, she would do anything to help him.

"I was afraid of this," Keelin murmured.

Under the dim light of the outbuilding, Kate noted her cousin's worried frown. "Afraid of what?"

"The McKenna Legacy."

"McKenna . . . you mean Moira's letter?"

Keelin nodded and quoted, "'Act selflessly in another's behalf, and my legacy shall be yours.' A double-edged sword, this bequest of Gran's. First I had to face grave danger...then Skelly...and now you. I fear that every one of us will be required to risk our very lives in order to find the happiness Gran wished for us."

Kate remembered thinking that she'd already blown her chance, that she'd been too selfish, that something within her had kept men from accepting and loving her as she was. But she couldn't tell her cousin all that. And what if the crazy Fates were giving her another chance? With Chase?

She asked, "Do you think the risk is too great?"

"No risk is too great to find the love of a lifetime. My fear is that we will not all survive the test."

Kate's heartbeat fluttered. Something to keep in mind. Sobered by the gentle warning and fighting the sudden anxiety that threatened to overwhelm her, she started for the house again. But by the time they set foot inside the door, Keelin was regaling her with a childhood tale that made her laugh.

On the surface, she smiled for her family's sake. But underneath, her worry festered. She tried calling Chase again and again to no avail.

She half listened to Keelin talk about the herb garden that had been Moira's and was now hers. Though she and Tyler would use Moira's old cottage as their second home, Keelin would sell her share of the herbalist shop to her two partners and start a similar business in the Chicago area.

Kate found herself watching the clock too closely. Fearing that something had happened to Chase, she grew anxious to leave for home. A quick change out of her flouncy skirt into more practical jeans and she would be off to the refuge to find him, despite her resolve to get much-needed sleep that night.

Finally she made her excuses.

Despite the chilly drizzle that had started some time before, Keelin insisted on walking Kate to her pickup. From the folds of her yellow dress, she retrieved a small cloth bag on a leather cord and placed it around Kate's neck.

"To help you make all the proper decisions."

"A medicine pouch?"

"Aye, something like that," Keelin agreed.

Kate lifted the cloth bag to her nose and sniffed. "How wonderful. What's inside?"

"Orange flower absolute to quiet your anxiety and to keep your heart calm. It also helps to battle shock and fear. Then there's rose to calm anger and keep your spirits up. Ylang-ylang will stimulate your senses and bring about a feeling of well-being." Keelin grinned. "And, oh, yes, considering where you're probably off to... ylang-ylang can also be a powerful aphrodisiac."

Kate laughed and wrapped her arms around her cousin. "Thank you."

They hugged for a moment before Keelin turned Kate toward her vehicle. "Go find him before you expire for the wanting."

Kate didn't waste time. A few minutes later, on the highway with windshield wipers squeaking, she brought the pouch to her nose again. Either she was a sucker for suggestion or the herbs inside were already making her feel better.

The euphoria lasted all the way home and up the wet front steps.

Expecting Wrangler to make silly noises when she placed her key in the lock, however, Kate was perplexed at hearing nothing. And when he didn't bark a greeting as she opened the door, she grew immediately concerned.

"Wrangler?" she called softly.

The mutt simply wasn't there. Every time she left the house without him, he escorted her to the hall, where he would be waiting for her when she came home. He was always in her way. Under her feet.

Except for now.

What was going on?

Not knowing whether she could safely enter, Kate stood in the doorway, her pulse fluttering wildly. What if someone had broken in to get to her and in the process had hurt poor Wrangler?

A weapon... something to protect herself...

Upon seeing the low flicker of light emanating from the living room, Kate immediately thought of the fireplace poker. Someone had not only broken into the house, but had had the nerve to start a fire! Her eyes were already adjusted to the dark. Trying to breathe normally, she moved into the hall and tiptoed its length before stopping again. Certain her heart was pounding loud enough to warn the intruder, she peeked around the corner.

Whoever had made the fire was lying on the living-room floor, his arm around Wrangler's neck!

About to fly to the fireplace and fetch the poker, Kate first took a better look.

The dark-clothed body on the floor was familiar.

She choked out, "Chase?" thinking he was hurt—or worse. For a moment shock rooted her to the spot, taking away her breath and stinging her eyes.

Then, with a responding groan, the body moved and the dog's head popped up. Wrangler gave a sharp bark and shot to all four paws, then shook himself out. As Chase pushed himself into a sitting position, Kate's pulse lurched, then steadied when he seemed perfectly intact. Yawning, he was trying to focus on her with what seemed to be little success.

He mumbled, "Kate, there you are," and yawned again. "Must have fallen asleep."

Tail wagging, Wrangler trotted over to her. Kate ruffled the dog's fur. Grateful that nothing had happened to Chase, after all, more relieved than she could say that he was still in one piece, she was also irritated at his high-handedness—letting himself in and making himself at home. Making her think the worst.

"What are you doing here?" she asked more sharply than she'd intended.

"Nice to see you, too," he returned. "I've been waiting for you." He rubbed a hand over his face. "I told you we needed to talk."

About the refuge of course.

Her adrenaline rush plummeting, Kate was chilled inside her damp clothes and boots. She moved closer to the fireplace and told herself she was not disappointed that Chase's being here wasn't more personal. Her conversation with Keelin had confused her, had made her focus on them, rather than on the more important issue. She retrieved the poker and used it to stoke what was left of the fire, then added fresh wood to the embers. Flames flared, illuminating the room with a flickering golden glow.

Disheveled from sleep, his dark hair tumbling over his forehead, Chase was nearly more tempting a sight than she could bear.

Kate's heartbeat refused to normalize and her throat was tight with confused emotion when she asked, "Do you want to go first or shall I?"

Giving her a strange look, he said, "I guess it doesn't matter."

"Fine. I was about to leave the refuge when Nathan returned from town." She fetched a couple of couch cushions and tossed them to the floor next to him. "I tried to stall him as long as I could, but I wasn't certain if you had enough time to finish your search. Did you run into him?"

"Yes, but—"

"So he caught you going through his things?"

"I was in his room when he got back, but I wasn't touching anything. Still, he knew. No doubt about it."

Not exactly what she wanted to hear, but at least the reality wasn't as bad as some of her imaginings. She collapsed onto a cushion, spreading out her skirt so it would dry faster. The dog lay down nearby.

"And he didn't threaten you?"

"Not directly."

Which meant the threat still existed, Kate worried. "What *did* you find?"

"That Nathan is more enthusiastic about being a Native American than you gave him credit for," Chase informed her. "Books about Sioux history and culture. Drawings of his people in traditional dress . . ."

Sensing he was leading up to something she wasn't going to like, Kate asked, "And?"

"And a trunk filled with artifacts of war—bow and arrows, a club, breastplate, shield, war bonnet."

The revelation took her breath away. And yet Kate hoped for another explanation. "They could be family heirlooms he inherited from his mother."

"If so, why would he keep them on the refuge, instead of leaving them at his place on the rez? He didn't have much else in that cabin, believe me."

"So what do you make of it?"

"Either Nathan's trying to atone for past disinterest in his own birthright . . . or he's gone militant."

That Nathan could be making war against the refuge over land that was being put to an altruistic use—if not the purpose he preferred—sickened her.

"But which is it?" Kate murmured, tugging at one of her new hunter green boots. It *would* have to rain the first time she wore them. And either the wet leather was being uncooperative or her nerves were shot, for she was having difficulty removing it. "Even if Nathan's guilty, he's not alone in this, Chase. Two of them are working together."

Her dramatic statement was backed by a crash of thunder and followed by a flash of blue light from the windows. The rain had picked up and was drumming against the side of the house.

"How do you figure?" he asked.

"Once Nathan left for the renovation site, I took a detour on the way home. I found Sage—"

He cut her off. "I thought we discussed that!"

His tone got her back up. "We discussed my not wandering around the refuge at night." The boot finally gave way with a jerk. "This was broad daylight."

"Semantics. I could tell you were up to something."

"I'm not that readable."

"Maybe not to anyone else. So you found Sage and . . . ?"

His implication that she was readable to him, added to his obvious annoyance at actions he considered dangerous, touched Kate. Even if he didn't admit as much, he must care for her on some level.

"I tapped into an earlier memory," she told him more calmly. "Before the stampede. *Right* before." Lightning lit the room again, reminding her of the vision. "I sort of know what happened to the mustangs that disappeared. We couldn't find them because they were hauled out in a truck."

The impact of her statement hit Chase hard. His mouth set in a grim line, he echoed, "A truck. Those horses could be anywhere now."

"Hopefully someplace safe."

"Don't be naive . . . and don't count on our recovering them."

"But the freeze brands—"

"Don't mean a thing to greedy people without scruples."

Kate didn't want to think the worst. "Maybe we can get them back before it's too late."

"Does that mean you know who hauled them out of here?"

She shook her head. "His flashlight blinded me."

"He? A man. You're certain?"

"Or a big woman. I didn't see a face. But I did see a silhouette. I'm pretty certain it was male."

Chase frowned. "Seeing this man and the rider responsible for the stampede doesn't mean two of our suspects are working together to ruin the refuge. One of them could've been hired help from the outside—most likely the truck driver."

But Kate didn't agree. "I don't think so. He never said a word and I'm pretty certain he positioned himself behind the truck's lights purposely so that Doc couldn't see his face. Besides," she said, starting to loosen the second boot, "Sage knew him."

"She told you so?"

Kate didn't miss Chase's skepticism. "In a manner of speaking."

"Too bad she couldn't give you a name."

Kate met his gaze. "She probably could if we wanted to put it to the test. Of course you'd have to get the cooperation of everyone involved."

"A lineup?"

"With a wild horse as the star witness."

"And a wild woman," he said, grabbing the uncooperative boot with both hands. "Brace yourself."

She set both hands on the floor behind her. "I'm not so wild anymore."

With a yank, he loosened the heel, slipped the boot off, yet didn't let go of her foot. "You could have gotten yourself killed."

"Everyone was busy." Aware of Chase's fingers around her ankle through the thick cotton sock, Kate was having trouble keeping her mind on her protest. Suddenly weak-limbed, she leaned back on her elbows. "No one was paying me any mind, and I didn't cut across the refuge—I took the long way around. Besides," she reminded him, "it was broad daylight."

"Which wouldn't stop a killer."

"I'd say whoever he is would be more likely to act at night. Chase, think about the number of horses missing. And that they came from various parts of the property. Whoever took them had to have made at least three hauls. What if they come back for more?" she asked as he let go of her ankle and propelled himself toward her. Heart racing, she continued, "Too bad we couldn't set up some kind of trap—"

Her sentence was cut off by his kissing her to the grumble of more thunder. Unfortunately the moment was over before Kate could close her eyes and enjoy it.

"What was that for?" she asked breathlessly.

"To stop your mouth before it talked your way into more trouble."

He was leaning over her, his weight resting on his hands, one of his knees wedged firmly between her thighs. The familiar plains of his body so close to hers fairly took her breath away. She flushed all over as her every nerve went on alert.

"Who says I'm afraid of trouble?" she murmured, thinking she was staring into trouble's eyes and liking it far too much.

"You should be."

"You want me to be afraid of you?"

"That's not what I meant," he said, his frown puckering the scar above his cheek. "You're misinterpreting—like the conversation we just had. When I said I wanted to talk, I meant about you and me.''

His serious statement sent a thrill racing along her spine. Tracing the small scar with a fingertip, she asked, "What about us?"

"That's what I want to know." Chase pressed his cheek against her hand and kissed her fingers. "Is there an us?"

Chapter Eleven

"You may not believe this, Kate, but I never forgot you," Chase went on, drawing away from her and sitting back on his heels. "I never really got over... everything that happened between us. When you walked back into my life, I thought I could resist you for your sake, but I was wrong. I'm not that selfless," he admitted. "The little sleep I get is filled with dreams of you. And when I'm awake, I want to be with you every moment. I know I disappointed you once. Can you find it in yourself to forgive me?"

"I already have."

She'd taken Keelin's question about which was the more important—a single deed or the whole man—to heart. There was no question that the man Chase had become was someone she could not only love but respect.

"You were right, you know," he said. "I was a coward. All those years ago, I had feelings for you that were more than I could deal with, especially considering the circumstances."

"You mean the accident," Kate said quickly, hoping Chase finally meant to be honest with her. She scooted into a sitting position next to him. "You've been holding this in for so long...I'd like to hear your version of what happened."

Maybe then she would truly understand.

Seeming torn, Chase finally nodded and settled down, keeping a small distance between them. "You'll remember we were putting up fences that day. I was already distracted, but if it wasn't for the whiskey—"

"I still can't believe you were drinking and working with heavy machinery."

"Stupid, I know. My judgment just wasn't there. We hit a rocky surface and the shaft kept spinning and getting nowhere. Gil decided to help the equipment along by adding his weight to the hydraulics."

"He got on top?"

His face drawn, Chase nodded. Kate took a deep breath. This was a detail Buck had never related in *his* version of the story.

"Buck passed me the bottle so he could help his brother. To this day, I don't know exactly what happened. I was in the middle of a long swallow when I heard the thuds. Suddenly there was yelling. I whipped around to see what was going on just as Buck jumped off the back end, then started shouting that his brother was caught and he couldn't free him. That's when I really screwed up. I panicked and somehow managed to put the tractor in reverse."

Kate's stomach clutched. "Oh, my God." She reached out to touch Chase's arm, offer him what comfort she could. He placed his hand over hers and continued.

"Then they were both screaming and I was being splattered with blood. Once I got the tractor in control, I jumped off and tried to help them. Gil lay there, his life's blood pumping out of him—a shaft blade had opened an artery. And Buck's leg was real messed up. Somehow I managed to haul them both onto the tractor, but by the time I got them back to the barns, it was too late. Buck was semiconscious and blaming me for his brother's death.''

"But it was an accident."

"I was drunk!"

"It sounds like you all were." Though she could understand why he felt guilty.

"I kept visualizing an angry lynch mob stringing me up, so I didn't hang around the ranch. And I couldn't wait until the next morning to find out if the sheriff would come after me. In the middle of the night, when I was certain my old man was out cold in a drunken haze, I sneaked out of the trailer and left Bitter Creek, vowing never to return."

"You were young." She herself had been horrified by the accident that had left one teenager dead and the other lame. But accident it had been, no matter the guilt from which Chase had run. "And we've all done things we have cause to regret later."

"Not like this, Kate. After you hear the rest of what I have to tell you, I'm not sure you'll want—"

She put her hand on his mouth. "Save it."

If he kept talking, he'd give her more opportunity to let the past come between them, and she didn't want that to happen. Not after he'd finally opened up to her. Her heart went out to him because she knew he was still carrying around the burden of guilt. If she could, she would remove it. The best she could do was make him feel better. Focusing on the rhythm of the rain drumming against the house, she feathered her fingers along his cheek.

"We'll talk about anything you want some other time…when we can't think of anything better to do."

Chase groaned. Gazing deeply into her eyes, he looked as if he was going to say something more, anyway. But in the end he changed his mind. His head swooped down, his mouth covering hers fully.

This time Kate took the utmost pleasure in his kiss, drawing out the interplay of lips and teeth and tongues. Eyes closed, emotions open, she shared with him her renewed sense of wonder. A woman now, she was no less thrilled by the thorough contact than she'd been as a girl.

Breathing hard, Chase broke the connection and made a new one as he buried his face in her throat. Sensation swamped Kate when he trailed his mouth along her sensitive skin—nudging her blouse out of the way—and lightly bit the delicate flesh between her neck and shoulder. His fingers tangled in her hair, and she felt him unsnap the clip that had been holding it out of her face. Now the natural curls tumbled around her shoulders in disarray.

Chase pulled back slightly, his hand coaxing her hair into an unruly mass. "That's the way I've dreamed of seeing you—wild and wanton."

"You should see me on a bad hair day," she joked, then swallowed her breath as, beneath her skirts, his hand slid up the outside of her leg.

"Mmm, and that scent you're wearing is almost as intoxicating as you."

Keelin's ylang-ylang, Kate thought.

Liquid heat followed the trail he broke with his hand. Kate responded by lying back and parting her thighs, allowing him more intimate exploration. She burned where his fingers found her and arched toward them for more. He tried to pull away the scrap of satin covering her, but the material wouldn't give. He slid the garment down her hips, sliding himself, as well, so he could follow the material with intimate kisses.

Finally he rid himself of his jeans, then lay back, and taking her with him, positioned her to straddle him.

She'd been wearing a skirt the night she'd been initiated into lovemaking, and Kate felt as if she was experiencing the memory the way she had when she'd tuned into Sage. Every touch felt like the first, her reactions that of an overeager and inexperienced girl. But when she eased herself onto him—they hadn't been quite so inventive that first time—she felt like the wanton he'd imagined her to be.

This had been predestined, Kate thought, unbuttoning his shirt, running her hands over his chest and down his taut belly. Their constant sparring had been a mating dance, a prelude to a joining that had been inevitable from the moment they'd laid eyes on each other again.

Even as she pulsed languorously over Chase, he continued to undress her. Slowly opening her still-damp blouse button by button, he watched through slitted eyes.

When he reached for the bag of herbs as if to remove it, however, she croaked, "No, leave that be." Whether or not it really held an aphrodisiac, she felt as if they'd both fallen under its exotic scent. No sense in breaking the spell.

As he slipped the blouse off her shoulders and down her arms, the tangled material imprisoning her hands, she threw back her head and closed her eyes. He thumbed her nipples through the satin covering her breasts.

Overcome with desire, Kate bit her bottom lip to stop from crying out. As if sensing her need, Chase rid her of the garments, molding his hands around her full flesh, while she began rocking her hips in the same natural rhythm as the beating rain.

She bent to kiss him. Their breaths mingled and grew heavier. A lusty sigh escaped her.

Waiting no longer, still buried deep inside her, Chase turned her flat on her back. She tore at his shirt, frantic to feel not only his bare chest against her breasts but the strength of his arms and the muscles of his back under her palms. She had little time to savor him before their passion exploded at the exact moment lightning lit the sky and thunder rattled the windows.

For a moment Kate floated, again visualizing that first intense glance when they'd rediscovered each other—until Wrangler's fearful whine and bark of alarm sent a chill through her.

She remembered that special moment had taken place at Doc's gravesite.

BUCK STOOD OUTSIDE the window, heedless of the rain that rolled inside his jacket and down his back. He'd had too much to drink to let a little rain worry him. And the naked bodies inside left him unaffected but for a growing resentment.

Chase Brody owed him.

He could have had a life.

A job.

A family.

Instead, he was left with a bottle in a paper sack. He took a swig from it. Whiskey dribbled down his chin, along with the rain. Chase's fault he was a shell of what might have been—a damn living ghost who'd been given a pity job by the man who'd crippled him.

Chase Brody owed him big time, would never stop owing him as long as he lived, Buck decided. Nothing would ever be enough for what he'd lost. Still, he would keep Chase paying for as long as it suited him. The guilt would keep the bastard from suspecting he was being duped.

Another swig had Buck considering new punishments. Especially one that would steal away Chase's humanity as Chase had stolen his.

Bleary-eyed from too much booze, he watched the couple inside hold on to each other like they would never let go again. Then he smiled.

The woman. That was his ticket.

Chase's losing the woman he loved would be the ultimate payback.

CHASE WOKE KATE at the crack of a drizzly dawn in a delightfully intimate manner. One body part led to another, and before she knew it, all thoughts of sleep had fled. The early-morning sex play left her ravenous, and she was surprised that Chase was talking about heading back to the refuge, rather than joining her for breakfast.

"What's the hurry?" she asked, pulling on a terry robe while he climbed into his clothes.

"I want to check things out," he admitted, "before everyone's up and around."

"You think something else has happened? More horses missing?" Kate's protective instincts were aroused. "I'd better go with you."

"No need." He played with a loose strand of her hair and kissed her on the nose. "I'm just being cautious. Who knows when they'll strike again?"

He'd said *they,* so he, too, believed more than one person was at fault. Learning that more wild horses were missing after the fact didn't exactly help matters, either. Not the horses, certainly. Kate was convinced there had to be a way to catch the rustlers in the act.

"I know it's impossible to predict *when* something is going to happen," she said, "but I was thinking of *how* we might catch them." Thinking about the day they'd found the horses missing had given her the idea. "You can see a pretty good portion of the north and west refuge boundaries from the old observation tower—"

"Too dangerous." Chase frowned down at her. "If I had the money or the manpower, I'd pull that thing down before someone gets hurt. You stay away from it." His hand worked its way under her chin, lifting her face to his. "Promise me."

Chase could be very persuasive when he wanted to be. Kate promised.

After he left and she had her breakfast, Kate went into Doc's study, Wrangler at her heels. The room was still overflowing, but she wasn't much in the mood to do anything about the clutter, even though she had a couple of hours before her first appointment. Besides, what was the rush? Happier than she could ever remember being, she swiveled in the office chair, her eye caught by the journals Doc had been keeping all his professional life.

Doc.

Her smile fading to bittersweet, she let her mind drift to his untimely death and the people who were suspect—nearly everyone they knew, it seemed, though she and Chase had concentrated on Thea Lockridge and Nathan Lantero. She wondered why he'd never figured on them working together, but she and Chase might be of like mind. Somehow she couldn't see Nathan giving Thea the time of day.

Who would?

Though she still couldn't envision Buck Duran hurting Doc, Chase hadn't eliminated him. Considering the difficulty Buck had had getting work over the years, he might be open to less-than-sterling methods of earning money. And no matter that he seemed to have forgotten the past, he did have reason to resent—maybe even hate—Chase.

Lying in wait for the guilty ones to strike was the only way they were going to learn their identities for certain, but how to convince Chase?

Leaning forward, she fetched the journal for 1978 from the shelf and paged back to the day of the fateful accident. Curious to know Doc's thoughts on the matter, she skimmed the passage relating the details of his working on Buck's leg and scanned the next few pages for a less-graphic follow-up entry.

Nothing caught her attention until another name fairly jumped out at her:

Merle Zwick came to me desperate for help. Nothing I could do for her but shore up the

bleeding and get her to a clinic in Hot Springs.
Poor girl. Two losses in as many days is enough
to break anyone.

Kate stared at the enigmatic entry for a moment, then
paged ahead, looking for another about Merle, but
Doc didn't mention her again.

Even back then she hadn't known Merle very well,
but Bitter Creek had always boasted a well-developed
rumor mill. If Merle had hurt herself badly enough to
be taken to a clinic for treatment, word would have
gotten around town faster than greased lightning.
Surely she would have heard something.

*Nothing I could do for her but shore up the bleed-
ing . . .*

Kate shifted uneasily at the ominous statement.
What if the bleeding hadn't come from an outer
wound? What if she'd been bleeding from the inside?
Doc almost made it sound as though Merle had been
having a miscarriage.

Two losses . . .

Losing a baby would have been emotionally devastating—if Merle had wanted to be pregnant. And
nothing of the sort had ever come over the grapevine.

A secret pregnancy?

But whose baby might it have been?

The possibility that came to mind spoiling her good
mood, Kate closed the journal and replaced it on its
shelf, wishing she had never remembered that Doc had
treated Buck. Then her suspicions wouldn't have been
aroused. She wouldn't have had another truth to learn.

She wouldn't have had the awful feeling that even
while Chase had been courting her, he'd been sleeping with Merle Zwick.

"No, it can't be," she whispered, emotions charged in a devastating direction.

But Chase had been trying to tell her something about the past before they'd made love last night. He'd indicated she might not want to be with him after he told her everything.

And she had stopped him, fearing the past *would* come between them.

As if he knew she needed some comforting, Wrangler nosed his head onto her lap. Absently she stroked his fuzzy face and scratched him behind the ears.

Two losses in as many days . . .

First Chase, then the baby?

Kate knew she was jumping to conclusions, but she couldn't help herself. The truth seemed clear enough for a blind person to see.

Kate wrapped her arms around Wrangler's neck, taking what comfort she could in his doggy devotion.

When Chase had run away without looking back, she realized, it was altogether possible that he hadn't left one broken heart behind, but two.

BY THE TIME SHE ARRIVED at the refuge later that afternoon, Kate was feeling a little more rational. Though she would make no accusations, she would ask Chase directly what he knew about Merle's plight. She only hoped he would give her an answer she could believe.

First she checked on Hercules and tended to his wound. That the infection was already showing signs of clearing pleased her.

"Feeling better?" she asked the gelding, rubbing his nose and giving him an entire apple.

He munched contentedly until a voice from behind her said, "You're spending an awful lot of time around here. Almost as much as Doc Weber did."

Hercules nervously shied away from the rail as Kate turned to face Whit Spivey on the other side of the corral fence. He was grinning at her, his rotten teeth as ugly as ever.

"If you'd rather have someone else vet your horse, just say so."

"A body'd think the refuge was more important than your private practice."

"Getting the lay of the land takes a while," she said, wondering where his conversation was heading. "And the place has had a few problems lately."

"None of your concern, though."

The flesh along her spine rising in bumps, Kate stared at the odious man. "Doc was my concern."

"The refuge isn't the safe place it used to be," Spivey said, moving away. He was heading for the lean-to and the handful of customers waiting for him. "I'd be careful where I stepped if I were you."

A warning if she'd ever heard one.

On edge again, Kate thought it a good idea to walk off her anxiety, so she headed for the visitors' center on foot. While wet in spots, the porous ground was free of muck. Not that she'd donned any of her good boots. She was wearing her oldest pair, the tobacco-colored leather darkened by myriad rains and snows. The heels had been replaced several times, the soles once. But she wouldn't get rid of what she considered to be her lucky boots—they'd gotten her through vet school. At the moment she figured she needed all the help she could get.

That was why, tucked beneath her green cotton shirt was Keelin's version of a medicine pouch. Kate reminded herself of its benefits—quieting anxiety, battling fear, calming anger, keeping her spirits up.

Fat chance! she thought gloomily, feeling sick again. *Merle and Chase . . .*

Please let it not be so!

Though the sky remained thick with clouds, they'd seen the last of the rain early that morning, and more was not expected until late that night. The gray day pressed down on Kate, a fitting match to the depression she was fighting, not only because of the entry in Doc's journal but because they were no closer to catching the people responsible for his death and the disappearance of the horses.

She still thought the observation tower was a good idea and meant to talk to Chase about it again.

Among other, equally disturbing things.

As she approached the visitors' center, Kate could see through the screened porch. Huddled together in the doorway of the office, Annie and Buck were having an intense conversation that seemed personal. Almost conspiratorial.

She shook herself. Now she was seeing demons everywhere.

"We can figure out the details later," Buck was saying, his tone intent.

Feeling a little odd coming in on their private conversation, Kate made enough noise opening the screen door to warn them of her arrival.

Upon seeing her, Buck nodded curtly to Annie and turned to leave, giving Kate the distinct impression that his sudden departure was directly related to her arrival. How weird. Buck had always been friendly with her. As he limped out of the visitors' center, he didn't even look her way.

Wondering what the surprising hostility was about, she stared after him.

"If you're looking for Chase," Annie said, "he should be back any minute now. He's at his cabin finishing that paperwork on the grant proposal."

"Thanks." Kate plugged the vending machine with enough coins for a can of soda. "I'll wait for him here if you don't mind." Though she certainly wouldn't talk to Chase about Merle where anyone could overhear. "Say, where's Merle today?" She hadn't seen the other woman around.

"She called in sick with stomach flu."

Kate sat and popped open the can, aware that Annie remained wedged in the office doorway staring holes through her. Didn't she have anything better to do?

Taking a sip of soda, Kate tried to remain polite. "Something I can do for you?"

"It's what I can do for you." The volunteer crossed the porch and lowered herself into the seat opposite Kate. Her expression was sympathetic as she qualified her offer. "If you want to hear the truth about Chase, that is."

Wondering what Annie was up to this time, Kate asked, "And what truth would that be?"

"An old one."

About Merle?

The entry in Doc's journal was obsessing her, perhaps because she'd already suspected Chase and Merle had a history together. She'd merely assumed that history had been a bit more up-to-date.

Kate took a big enough sip of pop to wet her suddenly dry throat. "Say what you have to say."

"This isn't easy. Buck was just telling me . . . Well, he's concerned that Chase doesn't hurt you a second time."

Never having been good friends with Buck, Kate wondered at his sudden concern, surprised, too, that he knew she'd been in love with Chase. And if he was worried about her, why had he acted so strangely just now?

"I'm touched, but I don't think Chase will be taking off without notice again."

From Annie's confused expression, Kate realized the other woman had no clue what she meant. Which meant Chase's leaving her in the lurch wasn't the topic in question. What had the volunteer hoped to share?

Back to Merle?

Taking a longer swallow of soda to hide her nerves, Kate said, "I'd appreciate your getting to the point."

"Yeah, sure." Annie looked down at some invisible spot on the table, her hair sliding forward to mask her expression. "Buck told me that when you were teenagers, Chase was never really interested in you."

Relief flowing through her, Kate laughed. "He could have fooled me."

"I know this isn't something a woman with any kind of pride wants to hear . . . but it's the truth," Annie insisted. "Chase bragged to his buddies about how someday he was going to have it all, including a girl who wasn't trailer trash."

Like Merle, she added silently.

Aloud she said, "That doesn't mean he didn't care about me."

"Buck and his brother bet him he couldn't get *you*. He took the bet, Kate," Annie said, lifting her head. Her blue eyes were filled with pity. "That's why he went after you in the first place."

Kate sat too stunned to say a word. Of all the things she might have expected Annie to tell her about Chase, his seducing her on a bet had not been one of them. And it certainly wasn't something she was ready to believe.

"Are you all right?" Annie asked. "I thought I should tell you before you got too involved."

Too late for that. Kate asked, "Are you certain you didn't misunderstand?"

"Sorry."

More to the point... "How do I know you aren't making this up?"

"Why would I?"

"Because you want Chase for yourself."

"Not anymore I don't," Annie assured her with a bitter laugh. "I gave it my best shot, but now I know I was fooling myself. And worse, I realize Chase Brody was never worth everything I did for him to begin with." Her gaze steady, she said, "If it wasn't for my loyalty to the mustangs, I would be packing my bags right now."

It all made sense in a sick sort of way, Kate realized, Chase and Merle being the real item, she the joke. Kate's heart twisted painfully. How did she know it wasn't true? Even now, having gone over everything that happened between her and Chase the night before, she couldn't be sure of him. He'd said all the things she'd wanted to hear but one. He hadn't actually said he loved her.

"You could be playing games with me," she said desperately. "So that I'll break up with Chase and you'll have a clear field...a chance to grab him on the rebound."

"I should have known better than to do *you* a favor." Her expression pained, Annie pushed herself up from the table. "Get real, Kate."

Without another word, Annie flounced outside, letting the screen door slam behind her.

Leaving Kate with the world crashing down around her ears.

HIS MOOD BETTER than it had been in eons, Chase felt his heart race when he saw Kate's pickup bounce along the dirt road toward him. About to get into the Bronco, he leaned against the door instead, grinning like a fool. He'd finally finished the damn grant request he'd been playing around with for weeks—maybe the papers would get the refuge some much-needed money. He'd worked on them like a madman.

Or a man inspired by love.

He waved as Kate pulled up. He shouldn't be so happy, not with the villain still on the loose, but she was enough to make any man smile. Not that she'd better try her wiles on any man but him, Chase thought.

Kate Farrell was his at last, and she'd better get used to the notion.

When she jumped out of her pickup, he immediately moved to kiss her, but Kate avoided his reach. "We need to talk, Chase. About us."

Immediately uneasy, he said, "We did that yesterday."

"We did a lot of things yesterday...some that I hope I won't have cause to regret."

He couldn't miss the edge in her tone or the way her green gaze had darkened. Her body language told him she was keeping a tight rein on whatever was eating at her.

His gut clenching, he asked, "Did something happen I should know about?"

"More like the other way around. Something *I* should know about. Actually a couple of somethings."

He was liking this conversation less and less. "What's going on, Kate?"

"Did you date Merle Zwick in high school?"

Not exactly what he'd expected her to ask. "Yeah," he said, relieved. "A few times. It didn't mean anything."

Her expression appalled, she demanded, "What you did to her—and your dating us both at the same time—didn't mean anything?"

"At the same time? Where did you get that from?"

"And going after me, seducing me, that was because you couldn't resist me, right?"

His mouth went dry. She knew. Why the hell hadn't he told her last night like he meant to? He shouldn't have let her stop him. Then he could have reassured her. Now it sounded like someone had confused her with nonsense about Merle, as well.

"Look, Kate, first of all, I always liked you—"

"Liked." Her face crumpled. "It's true, then. I was nothing more to you than a bet."

Sweat gathered around Chase's neck. "There was a bet, yes, but—"

"But what?"

"But being with you . . . I fell in love!"

"Of course you did. That's why you left town without telling me."

"Exactly!" Chase felt sick inside as he watched fury coil her body tight. "Because I was scared. I couldn't handle the adult emotions. I never told the guys that I slept with you, Kate, honest. I didn't collect on the bet, and I wasn't going to." Even as he realized her arm was shooting out at him, he continued, "By the time we—"

His words were interrupted by her fist finding his jaw and snapping his head back. Damn, she had some punch! he thought ruefully.

"Bastard! I thought you were a coward, but you were worse!" Eyes filled with tears, she said, "You were a user and a liar. You're lying now," she accused, "about Merle."

Gingerly he touched his jaw. It hurt like hell, but at least it wasn't broken. "What does Merle have to do with anything?"

"What does she—? She would have had your baby if she hadn't miscarried!"

"Baby?" Flabbergasted, Chase swore and tried to get hold of her, but again she thwarted him. "Kate, I don't know what lies someone has been telling you, but I didn't father any baby."

"Technically, no, because it didn't have a chance to be born."

"If Merle got herself pregnant, it wasn't by *me!*"

"You can look me in the eye and swear you never slept with Merle?"

His gut clenched. Chase only wished he could. "I can swear I never saw her seriously and certainly not when I was with you—"

Her tears cut through his words. Rivulets ran down her cheeks, and her eyes were so flooded he knew she couldn't stop. Kate never cried in front of anyone. Never.

"That's all I needed to hear," she sobbed, turning away and leaping into her pickup.

Feeling more helpless than he had as a kid when his father was using his fists on him or his mother, Chase didn't try to stop her. He didn't know what he could say to make things right between them. She had good reason to call him names. She would never believe he loved her more than life itself.

Sick at heart, Chase watched the only good thing he'd ever had in his life speed away from him, certain that this time, she was lost to him forever.

KATE DROVE SO FAST she had to clench her jaw to keep her teeth from clacking together when she bounced over the ruts in the gravel road. What a fool she'd been over Chase Brody. Even when faced with his lies, he couldn't be truthful with her. Angry with herself for letting him see her cry, she slashed at the trail of tears on her cheeks.

She didn't slow down until she was off refuge property.

Breathing deeply, she got hold of herself, but she couldn't put Chase out of her mind. Like some broken record, their argument played over and over in her head. She kept hearing him say he hadn't fathered any child and if Merle had gotten pregnant, it wasn't by him.

What if he was telling the truth?

How would she ever know?

Merle.

Of course Merle would know.

Kate wondered if she dared approach the other woman about such a sensitive subject. But how could she not? She had to be certain of whether or not Chase was telling the truth—though even if another man had fathered the baby, that didn't excuse Chase for the other.

Seducing her on a bet sounded so sordid.

But Chase had said he'd never collected, had never meant to. He'd claimed he'd fallen in love with her— words she'd longed to hear the night before. If he'd been honest about the baby, she thought desperately, then perhaps the rest of his explanation was true, as well.

Coming to an intersection, she didn't hesitate. She turned off the main road. Annie had said Merle was at home with the stomach flu. A minute later Kate found the mailbox marked Zwick and took the dirt road up a small rise. She parked her pickup, went to the trailer and knocked at the door.

No answer.

She looked around and realized Merle's pickup was gone. Undoubtedly feeling better after having rested all day—it was nearly dinnertime—the woman had left the premises. Frustration made Kate slap the door with the flat of her hand.

It creaked open.

"Merle?"

Maybe Merle *was* still home sick. Too sick to answer the door?

Perhaps she should check on her. Doc would...

"Merle?" she called again, louder.

Kate took a deep breath as she stared into the empty room. Her heart pounded as she realized what she was considering doing. She could check on more than the sick woman, Kate thought, struggling with the decision.

She respected privacy, had never before walked into someone's place without permission. But maybe something in the trailer would tell her what she needed to know.

Kate stepped inside.

The common room was neat. No dirty dishes. No piles of mail or magazines. Everything in its place. Not that Merle had a lot.

Sweeping her gaze around the room, she noted the single bookshelf and kitchen cabinets. Not places a woman would be likely to store a souvenir of the past.

"Merle?" she called again as she advanced to the bedroom. Empty. Kate stared. For a plainspoken woman who worked at a job usually reserved for men, she certainly did have her feminine, even sensual, nature. Satin bedspread. Heart-shaped pillows. Mirrored ceiling.

Shame stealing through her, Kate started to back out, intending to leave immediately, when an object on the nightstand caught her eye.

Hesitating only a second, she took the few steps necessary to pick up the object—a heavy ring, the metal band wrapped with yarn. The kind of thing a high-school girl might do so her boyfriend's ring would fit. She snapped on the lamp to take a better look at the high-school graduation ring dated 1978— the year she'd fallen in love with Chase. The year he and Merle had been seniors.

To Kate's everlasting relief, the initials were GD, not CB. She nearly cried with relief. It seemed Chase had been telling the truth about the baby issue.

As for the other...

Kate set down the ring and turned off the lamp, hoping Merle would never have to know about her little visit.

She felt the need to think things through alone before facing Chase again. And yet she didn't want to abandon the refuge and the investigation that was so important to its continued existence.

On the way back to her pickup, she thought of a way to kill two birds with one stone.

Chapter Twelve

"Do we flip a coin to see who gets you?" Hank the hunk asked as he and his buddies accompanied Thea Lockridge across the grounds, tennis rackets in hand.

"I prefer picking my own partner—in whatever sport I'm playing," Thea returned with a husky laugh. "I find things so much more satisfying that way."

"And I like a woman who takes charge," one of the other men mock-growled.

Kate waited until their voices trailed off, then left her hiding spot—some bushes alongside the outfitters building. Upon leaving Merle's, she'd driven directly to Lockridge Acres and had easily found the service road. The pickup was about a quarter of a mile back, hidden by a stand of trees. She'd walked the rest of the way.

About to commit her second crime of the day, she carefully looked around to make certain no one else was nearby to see her before trying the entry door. The knob turned easily. Unlocked, as she'd hoped. She slipped inside.

Getting into the gun room was a different story, however. Braced by a pair of mounted heads on either side—one elk, the other pronghorn antelope—its door wouldn't budge. Even if she could break the glass inset and stick her arm through to the knob, broken glass would alert Thea to an intruder when she returned.

Peering into the darkened room through the narrow window, she could make out a gun cabinet stocked with rifles and a couple of smaller wooden cupboards. In hopes of locating another window or vent unit that might give her an alternative, private entry, she checked the next room. All she found on the joint wall were bags filled with golf clubs and tennis rackets hanging from hooks.

The main room itself was lodgelike, two small seating areas flanking a marble-trimmed fireplace. The only other significant piece of furniture was a burledwood desk on which stood a large cut-crystal vase of fresh flowers.

Kate searched the desk drawers, hoping to find a key.

No luck.

She was wondering if she could figure out how to use one of the pins from her hair to pick the lock—they always did that sort of thing in movies—when she heard male voices almost directly outside the entry door.

"I need to get something inside."

"I'll stay here and finish my smoke."

"Be right with you."

Heart hammering, Kate dropped to the floor and crawled under the desk, praying the man wasn't planning on coming her way. Curled into a ball, she practically held her breath so as not to give herself away, but his footsteps led to the other side of the room.

Relieved, she uncoiled slightly and peered out from under the desk. The man's boots approached the gun-room door. He stopped and made a jingling noise. Since she could only see the lower part of the room, she couldn't tell what he was doing.

"Dammit!"

The grunted curse gave her such a start she whomped her head on the lower edge of the desk. Above, the vase rocked. Kate nearly panicked, fearing he'd hear, fearing the weight of the flowers would carry the cut crystal over and break it. But the vase settled and the man went on with his business. He shuffled a few steps from the gun-room entry, hesitated, then moved back. The scrape of metal on metal told her he was unlocking the door.

Thinking it might be helpful if she could see more of what was going on, she crawled out of her hiding place to peer around the desk.

Just then, the entry door opened and the second man yelled, "Hey, what's taking you so long?"

Kate flattened herself against the outside of the desk, trapped in full view if either man cared to look her way. Sweat broke out over her body.

"Forgot my key," came the answer from the gun room. "I'm coming."

The door slammed and the lock clicked in place. A few seconds' pause, and the man crossed to his companion.

"I'm so hungry I could eat a rattler. Got any plans for dinner?"

"Hey, I'm open to some company. Where to?"

The entry door closed, leaving Kate alone with the pounding of her heart and a trickle of sweat rolling down her spine. She nearly collapsed with relief. Instinct told her to get the hell out while the going was good. But even in her fright, she hadn't missed the man's reference to his key to the gun room.

If he'd forgotten his, how had he gotten inside?

Scrambling to her feet, she considered the gun-room entryway and wondered where the spare key to the door was hidden. The man had barely moved a couple of feet to the left. Her gaze shifted and met the glass stare of the elk. Her stomach tightening, she crossed the short space and reached up to move her hands over the mounted head.

"Sorry," she whispered, not unaware of the irony of its being the repository of the death warrant for others of its species.

Behind one of the antlers, her fingers hit something hard and out of place. The key went flying to the floor. Kate snatched it up and seconds later was inside the gun room, praying the storage cabinets would give her easier access than the door had.

The first cupboard opened without a problem, but to her disappointment, held camouflage vests and hats, rappeling equipment and balaclavas. Puzzled, she picked up one of the head-and-face coverings with openings for the eyes, wondering if the hunters really felt it necessary to hide their identities from the animals they were about to kill. Though to her way of thinking they should be embarrassed and ashamed of themselves, she was certain that was not the case.

A sudden loud noise directly outside the building froze her to the spot. Kate listened hard for a moment before deciding she wasn't being threatened with discovery.

Anxious to get the hell out of there and off Lockridge Acres, she exposed the contents of the second cupboard. Her gaze skipped over the shelves holding the smaller items and settled on the bottom where a half-dozen padded bags were lined up. Grabbing one, she unzipped it and checked the contents to be sure.

Eureka!

With the bag over her shoulder, she left the room the way she'd found it, then replaced the key with a silent apology to its holder.

Her success would be better than any apology, and if Thea Lockridge turned out to be one of the perpetrators, as Kate expected, providing the means for her own capture was another irony Kate could appreciate.

THE WIND SOUGHED between the buttes at the foot of the incline, the strange sad sound fitting Kate's midnight mood. Above, only the brightest of stars probed the gathering rain clouds, and the waning moon continually fought them to keep its place in the night sky. Sheet lightning ripped through the dark and danced in waves around her as if covering the sides of a bowl with her its center.

The wait had been interminable. She'd picked at her dinner until it had turned cold, after which she'd tried to sleep for a few hours only to dream of Chase. All in all, she was more frustrated than she was rested, not to mention disappointed that the man hadn't tried to find her, hadn't even called.

She fingered the medicine pouch, remembered the magic it had worked on both of them the night before. Or so she'd believed. Chase had told her his thoughts and dreams were filled with her. And he wasn't the type of man who gave up easily when he really wanted something.

So what was she supposed to think?

At least choosing to take action had given her purpose, as well as a good scare on her way to the refuge.

Despite the late hour, a vehicle had followed her straight out of town, and whether she'd slowed down or sped up, the other driver had kept an even distance between them. When she'd turned off onto a side road that ran behind the refuge, however, the other vehicle had continued south.

Until that moment she hadn't realized she'd been mentally holding her breath.

Her magnified view from the rickety old observation tower allowed Kate to see the better part of the refuge's north and west boundaries, either of which was a more likely horse-removal route than the east, which was closer to the main road and possible witnesses.

She was using the binoculars she'd "borrowed" from Thea's cache. Very special and powerful infrared binoculars that captured light from even the faintest of sources and multiplied it tens of thousands of times. The night-vision goggles probably made her look like some alien creature, but they operated hands-free except for the binocular function. The heavy headgear was padded for comfort and worked off a battery pack she'd strapped to her body.

Still . . . standing alone in the middle of nowhere in the middle of the night, buffeted by the rising wind and surrounded by erratic lightning, spooked her. She brought the medicine pouch to her nose and inhaled. As Keelin had promised, the fragrances soothed her anxiety, calmed her fears and renewed her spirit. She tucked the pouch inside her shirt, where she could feel it touch her skin.

Then she concentrated on her task, her enhanced gaze sweeping over the property.

She had a nearly normal view—as long as she didn't try to focus on anything that was too close. If she did, she might as well have been blind. For the first time, she could really empathize with a horse's inability to focus on distant and near objects simultaneously, the main reason for its shying at an unknown article on the ground while holding its head high and concentrating on some distant spot.

For the most part, though, the slightly distorted world around Kate was revealed to her in green-colored clarity.

A world alive with creatures more comfortable with the night than she. Coyotes. Owls. A cougar hunting for its dinner. Though the big cats were rare and kept to themselves out of self-protection—because of man, their numbers had dwindled—a few remained secreted in the hills.

And, of course, in every direction, she made out wild horses. Mostly the animals remained perfectly still, dozing while standing. But insomnia didn't seem to be peculiar to human beings. She'd just caught one mustang nuzzling another along the spine, a sure display of affection, when a crash from the opposite direction alerted her. Though she whipped around, she barely caught a hint of motion as whatever it was melded with a stone outcropping to the north.

Kind of big for a coyote, she thought, her stomach tying in a knot.

What then?

She didn't want to think whatever was out there could be human.

Uneasy, adjusting her binoculars to focus on that patch of rocks, Kate started to cross to the opposite rail. The wood beneath her foot protested. Stopping abruptly, she circumvented the weak spot, finding a safer route by testing before stepping. Looking down would only put her senses out of kilter.

Throat dry, pulse pounding, she kept watch at the west rail. She waited for a repeat movement—movement of any kind. All remained still but for tree branches wavering in the wind and lightning creeping across the sky.

Eventually her physical responses normalized and Kate let down her guard.

Her mind had been playing tricks on her, she decided, as it continued to do by drifting to thoughts of Chase. To whether or not she could believe him. Believe *in* him. She did believe in him when it came to his dedication to the refuge.

But what about to her?

Maybe she expected too much, which made it her problem, rather than his. She'd always known something intrinsic in her kept the men she cared about from committing to her without qualification.

Chase had admitted he hadn't told her he was leaving town because of fear. Given the opportunity, would he say he feared her now? Hard to grasp when she felt anything but intimidating or scary.

If only humans were as easy to understand as the animals she treated. Touch revealed their innermost beings to her.

Touching Chase left her in the dark.

As she walked around the perimeter of the observation platform, Kate had to back off weak spots several times. She was becoming edgy and bored. Sheer stubbornness kept her at her post. Kept her scanning the horizon for some indication of trouble.

At first she didn't recognize the lone horse as such.

The animal moved across the flat at a constant, if moderate, speed. Gradually Kate began to wonder where the rest of the band might be. And the route seemed predetermined. The dark bay was heading in a straight line, directly toward the northwest corner of the refuge. Directly toward the area that held the isolation corrals, which she couldn't see because her view of the flat there was blocked by rock formations and tall ponderosa pines.

Readjusting the binoculars, she brought the horse into focus and realized it was neither a mustang nor alone. A rider sat its back. A rider she couldn't identify, but one whose posture told her it was someone other than Chase.

Her head went light with the realization.

Tonight was the night!

A combination of triumph and dread spurred her toward the stairs. A five-minute drive would get her to Chase's cabin, she calculated. With a clammy hand, she hung on to the stair railing and kept her focus on the mounted horse, still too far in the distance for her to recognize its rider.

Together she and Chase would stop any more mustangs from vanishing.

Together they would reveal the identity of the person responsible for Doc's death.

About three-quarters of the way down the observation-tower stairs, it occurred to her that Chase might not be at his cabin. The thought gave her such a start that she faltered and misstepped.

The second she felt the wood give beneath her, Kate shifted her weight, but too late. Her foot slid through the opening and something sharp sliced her calf. She caught herself with both hands to keep from tumbling over. Or through the rotten wood. The rickety railing swayed with her weight, and Kate's efforts to focus on her situation only made her sick to her stomach.

Damn! Why hadn't she removed the headgear before taking the stairs?

Now she didn't dare let go of the rail to do anything other than free her pant leg, caught on splintered wood. One wrong movement could mean injury—or worse.

In the distance thunder rumbled a warning.

Blindly she felt for the fragments holding her fast, first removing the bit that still stabbed her. Pain shot through her calf. Ignoring the hot throbbing, she concentrated on undoing the damage, one splinter at a time.

At last she could move her leg if not free it. What was holding her now?

Carefully, eyes closed, she plunged her free hand through the break in the step and found the problem—another spike of wood had caught the material at her ankle. Her boot had prevented her from feeling it.

Freeing her leg at last, she was trying to stand when the sound of pounding against wood finally registered above a sharper clap of thunder. The sky lit—closer this time—and she saw a figure rushing up the stairs at her.

"No!" she screamed, unable to tell who it was.

He had his hands on her, was pulling her by one arm. She lost her balance and fell down several steps before regaining her feet. Who? Buck? Could the lame man move this quickly? Or was it Nathan?

Her hands flew to the headgear, but before she could loosen the straps holding the night-vision binoculars in place, he gave her another shove. She fell sideways, tumbling from one step to the next, stopping only when she hit the sandy earth. Winded, she tried to get up, but before she could manage to do anything but reassure herself nothing was broken, he had her by the scruff of the neck and was dragging her like an animal.

Rocks and trees careened around her. Even if she had the strength to fight him—which at the moment was a moot point—she was too disoriented to help herself.

As she tried to keep up with him to lessen the pain, Keelin's medicine pouch slid over her chest. If only it could help her now! She remembered her cousin saying that, to save Tyler's daughter, she'd called on power she hadn't known she'd possessed.

If only Keelin could see through *her* eyes... *That was it!*

Kate grabbed at the pouch beneath her shirt and concentrated. With all her conscious will, she sent her Irish cousin an American SOS, praying Keelin would receive it loud and clear.

And send help in the form of Chase Brody.

"I WON'T SPEND a night on McKenna property as long as James owns it," Uncle Charlie said while he paced the length of the Farrell family room.

Knowing her aunt Rose and cousin Neil were already sold on the reunion idea, Keelin smiled. "Then I've a solution. You'll be welcome to stay at my cottage. Da doesn't own it or the land, because Gran left both cottage and herb garden to me. Unless you've a problem with me, as well as with my father."

"No!" her uncle protested. "I think you're a fine young woman, Keelin. I'm very fond of you." He stopped in back of his wife's chair and rubbed her arm affectionately. "You remind me of my Rose."

Tyler was squeezing Keelin's hand, and across from her, Aunt Rose was beaming.

"I'm flattered, Uncle Charlie."

Keelin was thinking that her stubborn uncle was on the verge of giving way when a distinct impression coming out of nowhere intruded on her.

...rocks...trees...night sky tinted green...

"Keelin!"

...the sky pierced with white electric arrows...

"Kate?" Keelin whispered, shocked to her very core. "Is that you?"

"Kathleen?" Aunt Rose glanced around the room, looking for her daughter. Frowning, she asked, "Keelin, what about Kathleen?"

"I believe she's in trouble."

Keelin swiftly closed her eyes and concentrated, relaxing body parts, one after the other, in effect, hypnotizing herself. She quickly shut out the anxious voices of the people around her, registering them only as a murmur in the background...

HE SWUNG OPEN a door to the vehicle and pushed her inside. Her body fairly screamed with renewed pain. Vision distorted, she'd never felt dizzier in her life.

Keelin, please, please hear me!

Steadying herself with one hand, she shot the other to her head, but before she could rip the goggles from her face so she could identify him, he grabbed her wrist and cruelly twisted her arm behind her back.

About to give in to the pain and the despair, she felt it...another presence probing her mind...another pair of eyes seeing the same distorted images.

Keelin, thank God! She was so happy she felt like weeping. *Call Chase, tell him it's now. The isolation corrals. And tell him to hurry!*

As her hands were tied together, all she could do to help herself was repeat her silent message in case her cousin hadn't gotten it all the first time....

KEELIN OPENED her eyes to the concerned gaze of Kate's parents and brother. Tyler was holding on to her as if he guessed what she was about.

"What's wrong?" he asked softly.

"'Tis Kate. She's in desperate trouble," Keelin said, feeling dazed. Nothing like this—someone signaling and her receiving the message—had ever happened to her before. "I must be calling this Chase of hers."

"Chase Brody?" her uncle asked. "He's nothing to my daughter."

Not about to argue the point, she said, "Your daughter's life may depend on him."

"You saw..." Aunt Rose whispered, wide-eyed. "Like your grandmother used to, God rest her soul. The number..." She looked to her son.

Neil was already picking up the telephone.

AFTER WHAT SEEMED an interminable wait, the door opened and rough hands pulled at Kate once more.

She kicked out, but the man grabbed her leg, managing to get his hands around her wounded calf, and pulled her roughly out of the vehicle. She landed on her back.

She shrieked and yelled, "Bastard!" as much for Doc and the horses as for the pain he caused her.

"I told you she was trouble," her abuser said. "Followed her outta town and caught her spying, trying to set a trap."

"By herself? Untie her hands."

"So the bitch can gouge out my eyes?"

"Do it and get the truck!"

Recognizing both voices, Kate turned to face the rider who was far enough away to be in focus. A sad wind whipped between them. Though she'd considered the possibility, she hadn't wanted to believe it.

"I'm sorry it's you," she said as her hands were freed.

She removed the goggles and let them drop to the ground. The battery pack followed. Vaguely she heard the engine start and the vehicle speed off with a squeal of wheels. Dozens of mustang voices were raised in protest. More than one of the corrals was already filled.

The rider dismounted. "And I'm sorry you couldn't keep your nose where it belonged, Kate."

"You mean like Doc?"

"You may not believe this, but I hated his having to die. I didn't mean for anyone to get hurt but the one who deserved it—Chase Brody."

Not even the horses?

Knowing she was next, Kate pleaded, "Then stop now."

A bitter laugh was followed by "I'd rather be dead myself than rot in some prison. Hell, I'm already dead. Have been for half my life."

"And you want me to join you."

"All the witnesses will."

Kate looked past the mastermind behind the refuge's demise to the corral where the only true witnesses to Doc's death were trapped—Sage and her girls. Lightning bowled the area and gave her a long last look at the wild horses she'd grown to love. They were full of nervous energy, as if they recognized their fate.

Kate felt sick knowing they would be sentenced to a more ignominious death than she.

Chapter Thirteen

"Why couldn't you have left well enough alone, Kate?" Merle asked, holding her rifle steady on the nosy woman. Regret was becoming nearly as familiar an emotion to her as hatred. "Why couldn't you just accept the medical examiner's findings like everyone else?"

"I did. At first."

"Something changed your mind. And don't tell me the mustangs told you differently." Even as she spoke, Merle wondered if there could be any truth to the claim. But no. Then Kate would have pointed an accusing finger days ago. "Nathan gave me some cock-and-bull story about your being able to know what animals are thinking."

"What's your theory?"

"That Doc left something behind that made you suspicious."

Merle was fishing, hoping that if there was anything, Kate would say so. Then she would make certain to destroy any evidence. But Kate wasn't cooperating.

"How could you have killed Doc after he tried to save your baby?" she asked.

Startled, Merle drew closer. "How do you know about the baby?"

"Without Doc's help you might have died."

Remembering the horror of the miscarriage, Merle shivered. Or perhaps it was the rising wind that scraped at her. A storm was brewing, the likes of which they'd seen the night Doc died. She could smell the rain ready to fall. And the wild horses were getting spooked.

"A woman isn't alive merely because her body's still walking around after her heart's been cut out," she said. "I lost everything to Chase Brody."

"Chase didn't murder Gil."

"You know about him, too?" Doc must have told Kate a lot of things that were none of her business.

"I found the high-school graduation ring. GD, for Gil Duran."

"You were snooping in my things!"

How dared Kate touch the one thing she had left of Gil! The thing she'd stolen from the mortuary where he'd been laid out.

The damage to Gil had been too severe for there to be an open casket, so she'd broken into the place the night before the funeral to say her goodbyes. What she'd seen had been bearable only because she'd found his ring with his other effects and was holding on to it tight for comfort.

After that, fearing someone would take it away from her, she'd worn the ring only in secret. She'd worn it when she made love to other men so she could pretend they were Gil.

And Kate had violated that.

"You have no idea what it's like to love a man with your very soul."

"I think I do," Kate argued. "I love Chase the same way you loved Gil. But his death was a tragic accident."

"Your lover was drunk!"

"They were all drunk. All three of them should have known better than to work with heavy machinery—"

"If he wasn't guilty, then why did Chase run?"

"He was young and stupid. They all were, Merle. I think in your heart you know that."

Not anything Merle wanted to hear. She'd nursed her grievances for too many years to give them up now.

"Gil would have married me," she said as the first fat drops of rain began to fall. "We would have made a life together, and not in some damn trailer. My child wasn't going to be called trash like I was. I wasn't going to be like my mother..."

But she *had* turned out like her mother, bedding anything in pants, though not for money. That was Chase's fault, too. If Gil had lived, things would have been different. She would be different. Respectable. Noting Kate's expression of pity, Merle grew angry.

"Gil was the only one who ever took me seriously," she went on. "He died...then our baby...my grief over losing Gil was so intense I couldn't hold on to it...and I never had another chance at life."

"Because you didn't give yourself one," Kate argued. "How many people do you intend to hurt, or worse, before this is over for you?"

"I told you I was sorry about Doc...and you. I'm not a murderer. All I wanted was to take Chase's dream away from him. I wanted to destroy him emotionally the way he did me."

"But Chase meant you no harm. He meant Gil no harm. Can't you accept that?"

"No. And neither can Buck. You ask him . . . Oh, I forgot—you won't be able to."

"If you shoot me, they'll trace the bullets back to you," Kate said.

That was a crock and Merle knew it. "If I wanted to shoot you, I would have done it the other night. I did my best to scare you off." Again regret and something stronger—guilt?—nagged at her. "Why didn't you run and not look back?"

As usual Kate ignored her, asking, "Then how do you plan to kill me?"

"I don't plan on doing anything to you. I didn't do anything to Doc, either," Merle said, trying to convince herself. "He was in the wrong place at the wrong time is all."

"Like Gil was?"

"No! It's not the same thing!"

"Merle, it doesn't have to be like this. You can stop now. You can prove you're nothing like your—"

Not wanting to hear anything else that might confuse her, Merle lashed out with her rifle barrel to shut Kate's mouth. Metal clunked against skull. Kate's eyes rolled and her knees gave way.

She sank to the ground, quiet at last.

And Merle was still trying to convince herself she was not a murderer as she walked over to the nearest corral filled with restless mustangs and opened the gate wide.

CHASE PRESSED HIS FOOT to the floor. The Bronco bucked and twisted over the rugged terrain. Forget the roads. He was taking every safe shortcut—and some not-so-safe—he could think of. He couldn't get to the isolation corrals fast enough.

Keelin's call had taken him by surprise, but he hadn't wasted time arguing with her or denying anything. If Kate could talk to animals, he guessed her cousin could see through someone else's eyes. Besides, he'd heard not only the ring of truth in Keelin's words, but her panic, as well.

He only hoped he wasn't too late.

What the hell had he been thinking, letting Kate go off half-cocked? He should have tied her up until she'd agreed to listen, to believe that he loved her.

He could lose anything and survive it with the woman he loved by his side. But he couldn't lose her. Not again. No fool, he knew that losing her this time might be permanent.

Look at what had happened to Doc...

It suddenly struck him... the isolation corrals... the stampede...

Chase swore when he couldn't make the Bronco go faster. His gut was tied in knots, and he felt a searing pain where his heart should be.

He was so intent on speed that he almost missed the wash of high beams cutting through the night. Paralleling the road, the Bronco was slightly ahead of a sixteen-wheeler barreling in the same direction. What the hell was a truck that size doing on this road at this time of night...

Unless...

...Tell him it's now... the isolation corrals...

He hadn't exactly understood the first part of the message. But he did now. Kate had been trying to tell him that another roundup was in progress! The truck was on that road at that time of night because more of his wild horses were about to vanish!

Though it killed him to do it, he slowed a tad and made for the road, bumping up over the shoulder. A blast from the truck's horn told him the driver had spotted him. Good.

Chase pulled the Bronco directly in front of the sixteen-wheeler and purposely slowed even more.

More blasts cut through the night. Headlights flicked in his rearview mirror. Chase tapped the brake a few times and grinned like the devil himself when he heard the truck downshift. What a hell of a way to play chicken!

He repeated his maneuver until the sixteen-wheeler downshifted again.

Then, suddenly, it made a break, tried to go around him.

Ahead lay a treacherous curve with a steep embankment. Rain dropped like a curtain over the windshield. Flipping on his wipers, Chase took his chances, staying directly in front of the truck to distract the driver, only at the last minute pulling away. Through his mirrors, he saw the massive vehicle skid. The body jackknifed around the cab, and the multi-ton vehicle landed on its side.

Chase brought the Bronco to a screeching halt. Backed up. All the while watching for some sign of life crawling from the cab. Nothing moved.

Next to the immobilized truck, Chase stopped and hopped out. He climbed aboard the cab's side and peered into the open window as lightning danced around him, illuminating the interior. Wedged behind the wheel, the driver was regaining consciousness.

"Spivey!"

So the terrible things done to the refuge had been for nothing more significant than money, after all. The missing horses. More important and unforgivable, Doc's death.

"Get me an ambulance," the other man whined. "My ribs . . . and I think my leg is broken."

"Good. That means you won't be going anywhere." Though he had a million questions to ask Spivey—including where to find his wild horses—Chase had a more pressing mission. "Where the hell's Kate? Is she in danger? Who have you been working with?"

But Spivey was paying him no mind. Rather, he was blubbering to himself.

A waste of time!

Chase felt more than justified in leaving the bastard to suffer while he went after the woman he loved. Getting back into his truck, he heard the man's caterwauling above another rumble that shook the skies.

Maybe the pain would make Spivey contemplate his sins and some prison time. Hopefully a long enough sentence to fill in the remaining spaces of his lowly life.

"One down and one to go," he muttered, staring at a clear spot on his windshield. "Hang on, Kate, hang on."

KATE CAME TO spitting fresh mud, her ears filled with the squeal of an angry horse. Pushing herself to her hands, she shook her head and tried to rise, even as mustangs began milling out of their pens.

"Sorry, Kate!" came a voice through the fog of her headache.

Kate lifted her face to the wet sky. Needles of rain drove away the haze. Near the corrals, now open, Merle was mounted and raising her rifle. The sharp blast, added to an echoing crack of thunder, spooked the wild horses. They shoved one another, tried to jump over one another's backs in their panic to run from the threat. Merle squeezed off another round.

Freed horses ran blindly. She was in their path, Kate realized, fighting to get to her feet. Every inch of her hurt, though the pain would be nothing compared to what she'd experience if caught beneath the sharp hooves of several tons of horseflesh.

Heart pounding, she knew she couldn't stop them.

She certainly couldn't outrun them.

What she could do was pray she would be alive after they'd passed by.

Suddenly a mustang flew directly in front of her... stopping on a dime... nose pushing at her... squealing at her.

Dazed, Kate gasped, "Sage!" and realized the mare had come to her rescue.

Though she fathomed Sage had never been ridden, she grabbed a fistful of wet mane and launched herself upward. The nervous grulla danced sideways as members of a band that was not hers flew by, buffeting them, sprinting east along the road. Suddenly headlights shot out of nowhere, and the mini-stampede turned even as more mustangs freed themselves. Horses milled in confusion, butting heads, one going down in the fray.

Sickened by the animal's scream, Kate clung to Sage's back for her very life as the vehicle shot by them, then came to a screeching halt. She recognized the Bronco.

So did Merle, who, jostled in the confusion, was reloading her rifle with difficulty.

Chase flew out of his car, and Kate knew Merle would shoot him now that she was exposed.

Instinctively Kate thought to get to the woman to stop her, that wish seemingly transferring to Sage, who cut straight toward Merle's big bay. The mare showed her dominance, squealing and nipping at horseflesh to force them through the melee. As the gap between the women closed, Kate reached out to grab the rifle—her hand closing around the still-warm barrel—even as Merle tried to take aim.

"Let go!" a furious Merle screamed.

Kate jerked the barrel up, yelling, "Stop! It's over!"

They struggled for command of the weapon, both mounts dancing around each other. Kate eventually got a double grip on the rifle. With her free hand, Merle went for her face. Ducking, Kate gave the rifle a hard twist and tugged. The other woman refused to let go and, whether or not she did so purposely, squeezed the trigger. The shot renewed the panic around them.

Merle's bay leapt forward. Still clinging to the rifle, she lost her seat, her fall finally ripping her death grip from the weapon. For a moment triumphant, Kate looked around wildly for Chase across the sea of freaked-out horses. He was trying to find a safe path to her.

She yelled to get his attention. "Chase, catch!" Then she pitched the rifle to him.

Sage pranced around Merle as she got to her feet. Knowing anything could set off the herd again, Kate offered the woman her hand, but she refused to take it.

"I told you I won't rot in prison!"

Before Kate knew what she was about, Merle backed away, straight into the milling horses. A paint jostled one shoulder, an Appaloosa the other. She went deeper into their midst, buffeted but determined. Suddenly a current popped around them like a great electrical circuit coming to life. The land was thrown into blue-white clarity as sheet lightning circled them, followed by a crash loud enough to move the earth.

And the wild horses. A renewed stampede was on.

One minute Merle was there, the next minute gone, lost beneath hoofed feet.

Kate stared in shocked silence, even knowing Merle had been ready to die. Then the mustangs were gone, all except Sage, who quivered and complained but pranced in place. A few yards away, Merle lay still, covered with mud and her own blood, which the rain was already washing away.

"Kate!" Chase yelled, finally catching up to her. "Are you all right?"

Letting go of the grulla's mane, she held her arms out to him and was pulled into his wet embrace. Though every inch of her protested, Kate didn't complain.

Still gripping the rifle, Chase held her tight. "I thought I might be too late."

"Too late for Merle."

Freeing herself, Kate limped over to the downed woman and checked for a pulse to be certain. When she didn't find one, she gazed up at Chase through the rain and shook her head.

"I don't understand," he said. "Why?"

"Gil fathered the baby she miscarried, and Merle held you responsible for both their deaths. I'll tell you as much as I know," she promised. "But first we have to find Whit—"

"I already stopped him. Let's take care of you,"

"In a minute."

Though Sage had backed off, she hadn't fled. Kate slid both hands around the mare's neck and touched foreheads. Closing her eyes, she concentrated, mentally giving the mustang her thanks... *picturing Doc with smiling eyes and a happy grin splitting his beloved old face...*

As if she, too, saw, the grulla whinnied deep in her throat, backed off and, with a nod of her heavy head, whirled around and chased after her companions. Kate's eyes filled with tears as her gaze drifted to where the mustang that had gone down earlier lay in the muck valiantly trying to rise.

Next to her Chase said, "I'll take care of it."

She turned her back so she wouldn't have to see, but a shudder ripped through her at the rifle blast. Softly she began to cry for all who'd fallen because of Merle's twisted righteousness.

Chase put his arms around her waist and dipped his head next to hers. He held her and waited out her tears.

"I think they're all dead," she sobbed. "All the mustangs they took... Merle wouldn't have had the money to pay for help, and Whit Spivey's not the type of person who'd do anything for nothing."

"I've thought of that," Chase said.

Neither of them uttered the unspeakable, that the wild horses had probably been sold to some none-too-scrupulous supplier of horse meat.

Chase turned her in his arms. "How did you get Sage to let you on her back?"

Through rain and tears, she gazed up at the man she loved. "She offered. Isn't it amazing?"

"You're an amazing woman." He ran his knuckles along her cheek. "*This* is amazing. I can't believe I've found you again after all these years. If you can forgive me, that is."

"I already have," she said truthfully. When she'd told Merle that Chase had been young and stupid and had asked her to forget the past, she knew that was exactly what she needed to do. "The question is, how long do you plan on keeping me this time?"

"Forever... if you'll have me."

As Chase kissed her with more emotion than passion, Kate responded in kind, vaguely realizing their timing seemed predestined.

Why was she surprised?

In a world where touch allowed her to communicate with animals and her cousin to see through another's eyes, it only made sense that the grandmother from whom they'd both inherited their special gifts could work even more magic using the power of love.

The McKenna Legacy had offered Kate an inheritance she planned on cherishing for the rest of her life.

Epilogue

County Cork, Eire

On the McKenna triplets' sixtieth birthday, Kate and her cousin Skelly were sharing a few moments alone with Keelin between a buffet dinner and the official toast and cutting of the cake. Kate found the white-washed, thatch-roofed cottage Keelin had inherited from their grandmother as charming as anything she and Chase had seen in the past week. Delaying the honeymoon certainly had been worth the wait.

"Moira, my dear, thank you," Skelly said to the rafters. "You gave me the best inheritance a man could ever receive."

Knowing he was besotted with his wife, Rosalind, Kate smiled and admired the plain gold band on her own left ring finger. "Our grandmother knew what was important in life."

"If only finding our heart's desire did not need to be such a dangerous venture," Keelin said. "I wonder if Gran knew what we were in for."

"I suspect so," Kate said. "Nothing worthwhile ever comes easy. And we've all survived to tell the tale. We are her descendants, remember. Think of what a rich history we'll be leaving our children and grand-children." She looked to Skelly. "A history you could write."

"I've already thought about it," he admitted. "Though I might have to resort to fiction, since I doubt anyone will believe it's the truth."

Considering how complicated the truth could be, he was undoubtedly correct, Kate thought. They'd gotten details from Whit. It still saddened her that they'd been correct about the rustled mustangs' being sold to suppliers of horse meat that went into dog food. A horrific irony since that was the very fate the law was supposed to protect the wild horses against. But at least no one else had been involved. Whit had tried to enlist Buck, who'd talked a good game but hadn't actually carried out any action against the refuge.

As for the others...

A disillusioned Annie had gone back to Phoenix for good, saying she was going to try to pick up with the boyfriend she'd thrown over for Chase.

Upon investigation, it seemed Thea was running a secret society—her promises luring thrill seekers to the area—but wasn't actually staging illegal game hunts as they'd feared. The paramilitary stuff Kate had found had been part of an elaborate war-game scenario—most of the ammunition the sheriff had found consisted of nothing more damaging than paint balls. The cage had been part of the game.

Nathan had been the biggest surprise. Somewhere along the way to adulthood, he'd learned a new respect for his heritage. For years he'd spent any extra money he could earn on collecting articles of war, his goal to create modern artifacts using the originals for inspiration. And while he still thought the refuge land should belong to the Lakota, he'd done nothing to advance that cause.

"You'll have fodder for your novels for years and years," Keelin said to Skelly.

"How so, cuz?"

"You'll be remembering that each of us has two siblings, all of whom are part of the legacy."

"I can't speak for Donovan," Skelly said.

His half brother was the only one who'd refused to attend a reunion he felt had nothing to do with him. And unfortunately no one had been able to locate Quin. Kate couldn't help but worry that her younger brother was in some new fix.

"Don't you think we should be getting back to the others?" Kate suggested.

"You just want to keep an eye on that new husband of yours," Skelly teased. "Afraid he'll do a disappearing act on you?"

"Not anymore."

They strolled through the lush herb garden to the old limestone house. Indeed, this Ireland of Keelin's was a sight to behold. But already Kate was missing the Black Hills and especially the Bitter Creek Mustang Refuge and the cabin where she and Chase had spent the past few months together.

Keelin led the way into the house, dipping her fingers into the font of holy water and crossing herself. Their arrival caused a stir.

"Ah, here are our lost children," Great-aunt Marcella said, straightening the collar of her nun's habit.

"I was lost but now I'm found," Kate murmured as Chase pulled her to his side and kissed her cheek. Neil stood on her other side, next to their mother, while their father hung back, still a bit aloof.

Keelin joined Tyler and his daughter, Cheryl, who'd been getting better acquainted with Keelin's siblings, Curran and Flanna, as well as with Uncle James and Aunt Delia. And Skelly made faces at his stunning wife, Rosalind, who stood between his sister Aileen and Uncle Raymond.

"I cannot believe we are all reunited at last," Kate's mother said, lifting her glass.

Kate could hardly believe it, either. The warmth of happiness stole through her as she pressed closer to Chase.

"To the McKennas," Uncle James toasted.

"And the Farrells," Kate's father put in, finally stepping forward.

The two men eyed each other for a moment. Then Uncle James nodded. "Aye, and the Farrells."

"You'd best not be forgetting the Leightons, Da," Keelin said. "Now that I'm one of them."

"To the Farrells and the Leightons and any other who has the good taste to become a McKenna."

"Which, according to Gran's wishes for us all, will not be long in coming," Keelin reminded them, looking from her siblings to her unmarried cousins.

Everyone laughed.

And as they'd rehearsed it earlier, the three newly-wed couples lifted their glasses in unison. "To the McKenna Legacy."

HARLEQUIN®

INTRIGUE®

The Spencer Brothers—Cole and Drew...
two tough hombres.

Meet

Cole Spencer

Somehow this cowboy found himself playing bodyguard.
But the stunningly lovely, maddeningly independent
Anne Osborne would just as soon string him up as let
him get near her body.

#387 SPENCER'S SHADOW
September 1996

Drew Spencer

He was a P.I. on a mission. When Joanna Caldwell-
Galbraith sought his help in finding her missing
husband—dead or alive—Drew knew this was his
chance. He'd lost Joanna once to that scoundrel...he
wouldn't lose her again.

#396 SPENCER'S BRIDE
November 1996

The Spencer Brothers—they're just what you need to
warm you up on a crisp fall night!

Look us up on-line at: http://www.romance.net

TSB

MILLION DOLLAR SWEEPSTAKES

SWP-M96

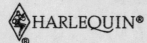 

REBECCA

43 LIGHT STREET

YORK

FACE TO FACE

*Bestselling author Rebecca York returns to "43 Light Street"
for an original story of past secrets, deadly deceptions—and
the most intimate betrayal.*

She woke in a hospital—with amnesia...and with child.
According to her rescuer, whose striking face is the last
image she remembers, she's Justine Hollingsworth. But
nothing about her life seems to fit, except for the baby
inside her and Mike Lancer's arms around her. Consumed
by forbidden passion and racked by nameless fear, she
must discover if she is Justine...or the victim of some mind
game. Her life—and her unborn child's—depends on it....

Don't miss *Face To Face*—Available in October, wherever
Harlequin books are sold.

HARLEQUIN ®
®

43FTF

Free Gift Offer

With a Free Gift proof-of-purchase
from any Harlequin® book, you can receive
a beautiful cubic zirconia pendant.

This stunning marquise-shaped stone is a genuine cubic
zirconia—accented by an 18" gold tone necklace.
(Approximate retail value $19.95)

Send for yours today...
compliments of HARLEQUIN®

To receive your free gift, a cubic zirconia pendant, send us one original proof-of-purchase, photocoples not accepted, from the back of any Harlequin Romance®, Harlequin Presents®, Harlequin Temptation®, Harlequin Superromance®, Harlequin Intrigue®, Harlequin American Romance®, or Harlequin Historicals® title available in August, September or October at your favorite retail outlet, together with the Free Gift Certificate, plus a check or money order for $1.65 U.S./$2.15 CAN. (do not send cash) to cover postage and handling, payable to Harlequin Free Gift Offer. We will send you the specified gift. Allow 6 to 8 weeks for delivery. Offer good until December 31, 1996, or while quantities last. Offer valid in the U.S. and Canada only.

Free Gift Certificate

Name: _____

Address: _____

City: _____ State/Province: _____ Zip/Postal Code: _____

Mail this certificate, one proof-of-purchase and a check or money order for postage and handling to: HARLEQUIN FREE GIFT OFFER 1996. In the U.S.: 3010 Walden Avenue, P.O. Box 9071, Buffalo NY 14269-9057. In Canada: P.O. Box 604, Fort Erie, Ontario L2Z 5X3.

FREE GIFT OFFER   084-KMFR
ONE PROOF-OF-PURCHASE
To collect your fabulous FREE GIFT, a cubic zirconia pendant, you must include this
original proof-of-purchase for each gift with the properly completed Free Gift Certificate.

Merry Christmas, Baby!

A romantic collection filled with the magic of Christmas and the joy of children.

SUSAN WIGGS, Karen Young and Bobby Hutchinson bring you Christmas wishes, weddings and romance, in a charming trio of stories that will warm up your holiday season.

MERRY CHRISTMAS, BABY! also contains Harlequin's special gift to you—a set of FREE GIFT TAGS included in every book.

Brighten up your holiday season with *MERRY CHRISTMAS, BABY!*

Available in November at your favorite retail store.

HARLEQUIN ®

®

MCB

You're About to Become a *Privileged Woman*

Reap the rewards of fabulous free gifts and benefits with proofs-of-purchase from Harlequin and Silhouette books

Pages & Privileges™

It's our way of thanking you for buying our books at your favorite retail stores.

PROOF OF PURCHASE
HI-PP183
Offer expires October 31, 1996

Pages & Privileges ™

Harlequin and Silhouette—
the most privileged readers in the world!

For more information about Harlequin and Silhouette's PAGES & PRIVILEGES program call the Pages & Privileges Benefits Desk: 1-503-794-2499

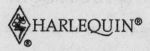

HARLEQUIN®

HI-PP183